Maureen Murphy Williams

CINCO

DE

MEOW

A Mo the Shelter Cat Mystery

Cinco de Meow
A Mo the Shelter Cat Mystery
All Rights Reserved
Copyright @ 2015 Maureen Murphy Williams

Cover photo @2015 Gordon Gutchess. All rights reserved - used with permission.

Catmandu Books

ISBN: 9780692520260

Acknowledgments

Since each of us is blessed with only one life, why not live it with a cat? *Robert Stearns*

Morgan (Mo), the inspiration for this cat detective series, was a longtime shelter resident. Much of her three-year stay in shelters was spent at the Cat Adoption Team in Sherwood, Oregon. The patience, compassion and love shown by staff in shelters everywhere are just a few of the reasons cats in shelters are able to thrive, and that so many homeless animals are placed in loving homes.

CAT and I hope Morgan's story will inspire more people to help a shelter animal. A portion of the Mo the Shelter Cat Mystery series book sales is pledged to CAT for all they do. You can check CAT out at: www.catadoptionteam.org.

MO

IMPORTANT FELINE CHARACTERS

MO

A beautiful gray and white feline whose proper name is Morgan; came to the shelter when her 'mum' was murdered. Our feline heroine, companion to Kate Ferguson and Ambassador to Cats Pause Feline Shelter. Mo also serves as the Winery Cat for Kats Jory Hills Estate Vineyard and Winery, a duty she takes seriously even though grapes are not included among her favorite culinary indulgences.

MONA, MAC and MURPHY

A former feral Tiger mom and her two Maine Coon offspring. Adopted and adored by Yamhill County Commissioner George King. Although sleuths by nature, these

i

three have their hands full with George, who always manages to find himself in the center of trouble in Yamhill County.

LADY and *SEÑOR*

Two feral cats rescued by Olivia Knightly. Now enjoying a world of barn mousing and home life at Andrew Knightly's horse ranch.

GEORGIA

A beautiful midnight black feline. Found her purr-fect family with Rebecca Sherlock and Rebecca's new baby, Lawrence Junior. Georgia and Mo were instrumental in finding Lawrence Senior's murderer in Seven Oaks, Oregon.

SQUEAKER and *WINSTON*, two shelter cats adopted by Olivia Knightly to join *LADY and SEÑOR* at the Knightly Ranch, where they will collude with their fellow felines in the arts of mousing and human-keeping.

ANDREW and *SARAH,* appropriately nicknamed *ARBOR* and *SYRAH,* named as a tribute to vineyards everywhere. "Belong" to veterinarian, James Middleton. These two are the veterinary clinic greeters, exuding relaxation and contentment to stressed feline clinic patients.

DIANA and *EDWARD,* beautiful Siamese and handsome Tuxedo cats respectively. A lovely pair who reside with the Kensingtons and their daughters, Pippa and Beatrice. These nice humans arrange kitty visits with *PHILLIP,* a dashing gray, brown and black Maine Coon with only one seeing eye, now in his furr-ever home with Elizabeth Conley. These three former orphaned felines consoled Morgan upon her arrival at Cats Pause after her mum was murdered, and helped Mo find the killer and her place as the centerpiece in Kate's heart.

VICTORIA, black kitten rescued from a delivery truck by *LADY AND SEÑOR,* temporarily residing indoors with Olivia Knightly at her horse ranch. Because *VICTORIA* is lonely for a feline companion of her own, her friends search for the perfect mate or cohort.

IMPORTANT HUMAN CHARACTERS

Kate Ferguson

Director of Cats Pause Feline Shelter and champion for felines in and around Seven Oaks, Oregon. Proud adopted 'mum' to *MO*. Proprietor of Kats English Bed and Breakfast, her lifetime dream, a B&B establishment located on her father's property, Kats Jory Hills Estate Vineyard and Winery.

Lt. Charles Beltz

Community Services Coordinator, Yamhill County police department detective. Friend (and more) to Kate.

James Middleton

Local veterinarian, proprietor of The Cats Meow Clinic. Da' to *ARBOR* and *SYRAH*.

Mary Malone

James' veterinarian's assistant (and more?) at The Cats Meow Clinic. Kate's best friend.

Olivia Knightly

Volunteer at Cats Pause, mum to *LADY* and *SEÑOR* and new mum to *WINSTON and SQUEAKER.* Daughter of Andrew Knightly and good friend to Donald Jenkins who worked with the horses on her father's ranch.

Andrew Knightly

Olivia's father, owner of The Knightly Ranch, raises champion Tennessee Walking Horses and keeps a small vineyard.

Donald Jenkins

Farmhand, horse trainer and friend to Andrew and Olivia at the Knightly Ranch.

John Ferguson

Kate's father. Owner of Kats Jory Hills Estate Vineyard and Winery.

Victoria Malone

Mary Malone's older sister, a quilter by trade. Volunteer at Cats Pause.

George King

Editor of the *Jory Hills Times*, a Yamhill County Commissioner and da' to *MONA*, *MAC* and *MURPHY*.

Rebecca Sherlock

Owner of the gathering and reunion business, "Let's Get Together." 'Mum' to *GEORGIA* and new arrival, Lawrence Junior and widow of Lawrence Senior.

Elizabeth Conley

Proprietress of burgeoning business, The Print Shoppe. Purr-fect match for *PHILLIP*, her adopted lifetime feline companion. Perhaps *PHILLIP* will not be lonely when Elizabeth is working if he can convince her to welcome a companion to keep him company. Which lucky feline will become *PHILLIP'S* cohort?

Duke Loma

New part-owner of Western Hay and Grain's business.

William Kent

Kats Jory Hills Estate winemaker. Lobbyist for vineyards and wineries in the Jory Hills American Viticultural Area (AVA).

Jaime, Juan and Paco

Ranch workers (cowboys) at the Knightly Ranch.

The Kensingtons

A very nice couple, with daughters,
Beatrice and Pippa. Purr-fect matches to
DIANA and *EDWARD.*

x

CINCO DE MEOW

Chapter 1 –

Civilization is defined by the presence of cats. *Unknown*

The last memory Donald Jenkins would ever have was the calm and painless manor in which he died. How could this happen? He didn't believe for a moment that it was his time. Yet, here it was: the inevitable cycle had been foreclosed even though he felt in his prime.

But this event was not by accident, nor by natural cause.

Donald was simply doing his job, tending to the horses in the early morning at the Knightly Ranch. He loved everything about the horses, their smell, the graceful lines of their flanks and proud manes and tails as they cavorted in the paddocks, the whinnies that greeted him when he approached them in the barn or in the fields as they grazed.

And Donald loved his employer. No one had been more kind to him than Andrew Knightly. Donald had a prison record. But he was a kind man and a hard worker, and even though he had fallen onto bad circumstances, he had redeemed himself to the extent that he had only served three years of a ten-year sentence. When he was released, though, the reformed ex-prisoner couldn't find a job. When he approached Andrew at the Knightly Ranch seeking farm labor, he was prepared yet again for rejection.

But Andrew recognized a man for his worth, so he hired Donald and made him part of the ranching family. Andrew would say that he never for a moment regretted that decision, a sentiment that Donald had endlessly appreciated. And Olivia! She was such a joy to be around, and she had a gift with the animals. She reminded him of a horse whisperer, except that she understood ALL the animals, though especially the horses and cats. She had endeared herself to Donald as no "child" ever had, perhaps due to having none of his own. But if he'd had a child, he wished the child to be exactly like Olivia.

Then what had he done to deserve *this*? He had committed a very stupid, worthless crime while still in his 20's. He had asked for forgiveness every day when he awoke, and he had vowed each day to become the kind of man who would make his father proud. No one worked harder, gave more back or was more compassionate than Donald Jenkins.

Someone, however, didn't care that Donald had reformed and had become the good man he was meant to be. Someone wanted him dead. The knife placed precisely in Donald's heart was accomplishing just that.

How he would miss this life! There was so much more to do, so much more he needed to repay! But as his life ebbed away, the murderer slipped into the shadows and Donald was left to die far out in the fields among the horses he so loved.

Chapter 2 –

There is no cat 'language.' Painful as it is for us to admit, they don't need one. *Barbara Holland*

Given the dynamics of planning an event, especially at a winery, Kate Ferguson knew that she had to leap headlong into the matter.

She had only a few days to make everything perfect, as the Fifth of May was rapidly approaching and the particular holiday – Cinco de Mayo – wine tasting event was a huge draw for wineries in Yamhill County. It also served as a precursor to the Memorial Day Weekend wine tours, one of the two biggest wine events of the year, second only to Thanksgiving Weekend.

CINCO DE MEOW

People who loved the ambiance and wines featured at a Cinco de Mayo event at a particular winery, would return on Memorial Weekend, and would bring friends and guests to enjoy tasting and to make wine purchases, to join wine clubs and to make glowing recommendations to other friends, as well.

Since Kate's father, John Ferguson had completed his winery and tasting room, they could schedule their first open house to feature their wines, and of course, some of the wonderful Mexican foods catered from several ethnic restaurants in Seven Oaks and McMinnville, Oregon.

While John and his winemaker, William Kent continued the daunting task of organizing wines to serve at the open house, completing the bottle labeling of the most recent vintages and pulling kegs from which to offer keg tasting – newer wines not yet ready for bottling – Kate would be the event coordinator, responsible for advertising, registration and ticket sales, and for creating the flavor of the event itself.

Assisting her with more than her share of local savvy, Kate's best friend, Mary Malone was the perfect example of efficiency. Mary was the mainstay and manager at the Cats Meow

Veterinary Clinic, she volunteered many hours at Cats Pause Feline Shelter and she now offered her unique design and culinary acumen to complement the Mexican holiday flavor of the upcoming event.

Morgan, or Mo as she was called by her many friends, had spent the night at Cats Pause, where when not performing her duties as the vineyard/winery cat, she served as ambassador for and liaison between the shelter cats and potential adopters in the Seven Oaks area. A beautiful gray and white feline girl with spider-web-like markings on her generous flanks, Mo was sensitive to remarks about her size. Well, she was a large cat, but upon hearing any discussion regarding her weight, she would simply hiss, turn her tail and walk away. That hiss, of course, meant *I'm big-boned with excellent muscle tone* in cat speak. With hypnotizing green eyes and an extremely expressive countenance, especially when indignant or bored, Mo had many friends, both feline and human.

CINCO DE MEOW

Morgan

As director of Cats Pause Feline Shelter, Kate relied upon Morgan's soothing and sensible qualities to calm newly arrived abandoned and orphaned cats and to help prepare all of the shelter cats for introductions to new families. Their goal was to match appropriate feline 'cattitudes' with unique human attitudes to ensure a happy and forever union. Many kittens were starting to arrive at the shelter, as spring-to-early-summer was kitten birth season. Kate and Mo were quite perplexed that so many cat parents still refused to spay and neuter their charges.

Of course, many of these kittens were born to strays or to ferals, and capturing the momma cat was integral to both nurturing the kittens until they could be weaned, and neutering the momma and the kittens so this unfortunate event could never occur again – at least to those particular felines. Many times, momma cat was not feral; rather she was an abandoned, once-domestic cat who had become a stray cat. She, too, needed to be neutered and to find a new home with loving humans. Those felines who would not thrive in domestic situations were returned to their clowders if the clowder or group had a caretaker.

But the most remarkable facet of the Mo-Kate union was that they shared an unusual form of communication – 'telepathy.' On more than one occasion, one had signaled the other to provide vital information – or simply to say goodnight or good morning. However, Kate strove to keep that talent as best as possible between herself and Mo because few people really believed that could happen. A cat 'talking' with a human and vice versa was unimaginable, highly unlikely at best.

As time went on, however, it became rather clear to friends and family that there was, indeed, an extraordinary communication at work between the two, even though the probability of translation of the two languages was still too far-fetched to be believable.

The fact that the cats talked with one another and understood each other clearly was also lost on most people. Kate, however, was absolutely certain that the cats knew how to communicate and felt comfort in that thought, especially with respect to the comforting element that communication offered between the shelter cats.

This morning, though, Mo was beginning to feel uneasy, and somehow the natural sleuth trait inherent in most cats was taking over Mo's psyche.

Chapter 3 –

The problem with cats is that they get the same exact look whether they see a moth or an axe murderer. *Paula Poundstone*

Cats have earned that "curious as a..." handle honestly. Mo had overheard Olivia Knightly, her favorite shelter volunteer who always arrived very early, confide to visiting veterinarian, James Middleton that her horses had become agitated in the early morning hours, whinnying and carrying on so that Olivia had gone out to the barns to calm a few of them down. Since she couldn't locate the horse trainer Donald Jenkins in the barn, Olivia assumed he was out in the pasture attending to several of the horses. But adding to her unease, Olivia's two rescued ferals, Lady and Señor had followed her to the barn and had piped in with howling that she swore would wake the dead. That alarmed Mo, too. Mo knew Olivia's two kitties well, and also knew they were very sensitive to odd, unusual or sometimes dangerous vibrations, the kind that cats – and only some dogs – can distinguish.

Curiosity won't kill this cat! Something's amiss, and I need to find my way to Olivia's ranch, thought Mo. *Kate, please come to the shelter and pick me up so we can go to the Knightly ranch. I fear someone may need our help!*

At the winery, Kate flinched slightly as she set a case of wine goblets behind the tasting bar. *What now, Mo? I left the B&B early and I'm in the middle of the Serving Phase of planning the Cinco de Mayo event and I'd like to complete this portion before I move on to something else.*

Mum, Lady and Señor were upset and howling this morning, and Olivia says the horses were spooked, too. You know very well that horses and cats sense danger and impending disaster better than humans can. I have a very bad feeling about this, and we need to see whether someone needs us as I sense they do.

Shaking her head so that her auburn hair swished against her face, Kate resigned herself to the task. Oh all right, Mo. I'll be right there. I do trust your instincts and if someone needs our help, we must go to them.

"Mary," offered Kate as she set down another box of wine glasses, "I need to check in at the shelter. Can you take over here until I get back? I was just about to bring in a few more cases of wine goblets to store behind the tasting bar."

"Of course," replied Mary. "But on my way here just a short time ago, I stopped by the shelter briefly to drop off some clean towels and blankets. Everything seemed fine then, and Olivia and my sister, Victoria, had just arrived and were already hard at work feeding the felines some new delectable morsels and cleaning their apartments. Victoria is just loving her new 'job' and I've noticed she spends more time at the shelter than she does working on the quilting skills she inherited from our mother. Did either of them call you?"

"No," confessed Kate, "but although I completely trust your assessment of the shelter status, I always feel strange when I don't start my day by doing my own assessment – and petting every single head in the place to let them know someone cares. I should make sure the Cat Food Community Barrels and the supplies of shelter cat food have been replenished, too. I also like to be sure the volunteers are comfortable with handling everything and that the numbers of visitors do not overwhelm the volunteers – as they have several times lately. I am so thrilled that our temporary residents have garnered so much interest from families wishing to adopt. Let's hope we can maintain that momentum at the shelter. Why, yesterday, we had two new arrivals, kittens, and they were added to a population of fifty cats awaiting homes. I do recall the days when thirty or forty temporary residents at the shelter were not uncommon, but since we've expanded, we have more room to welcome cats for temporary residence.

I recently received a notice that some of the larger shelters in Oregon are welcoming abandoned and orphaned felines from high-mortality shelters in Hawaii and California. I wish we had even more room to take in a few cats from other shelters. I will say, though, the larger shelters have much success placing the out-of-state arrivals since they are usually located in more densely populated regions. They do a bang-up job of exposing these orphans to potential adopters through social media. I wish I had the photographic skills that I see in some of the online pictures. Those talented individuals capture the very essence of each animal they photograph."

Kate finished by cleaning the countertop and said her goodbyes to Mary as she closed the tasting room door. Once outside in the bright sunshine of the Yamhill Valley spring day, she unlocked the driver's door of the Mini. Kate loved driving the Mini Cooper S. The little sprite responded so quickly and quietly to her touch, yet it performed like a new Jaguar on the road.

She pulled into the parking lot of Cats Pause, parked the Mini, and almost sprinted to the lobby to retrieve Mo. The outside of the shelter was blooming – literally. Due to an unseasonably warm winter, spring had arrived several weeks earlier than usual this year, and buds and flowers were abundant everywhere. While the yellows and purples accented the former residential cottage, now Cats Pause Feline Shelter, the red tulips literally popped against the pale yellow exterior of the shelter and the surrounding white picket fence.

Kate felt a bit guilty for having told Mary that she was worried about the shelter. She would make amends later and certainly she would return to the shelter shortly to accomplish all the tasks she had mentioned to Mary as having beckoned her on this trip.

Kate waved to Olivia and Victoria, swooped into her office, and plucked Mo from her desk top where Mo had dragged a small towel to cuddle in. She said "Good morning, Mo!" and cradled her in her arms for the short trek out to the car. No small feat considering Mo weighed in at eighteen pounds.

Mo did not particularly like to ride in the red faux fur-lined carrier Kate kept in the Mini. She preferred to sit on the shelf that rested behind the seat; it was situated at headrest level and she could literally see the world rushing by. But Kate insisted on the safety of the carrier when they were going out into the countryside or onto the highway, so Mo had resigned herself to riding in the contraption. Many times, Kate would allow Mo to bring along a friend from the shelter, especially if Mo was mentoring a newly arrived feline who was not yet comfortable being alone with visitors. Today was different, and Mo was dispatched with little ceremony to the kitty carrier amid her sighs of displeasure.

They drove in silence the few miles to Knightly's horse ranch, and by the time they arrived, it had clouded over again and begun to shower, as it often does in the mid-valley springtime. March, April and May hold much moisture for the valleys, soaking that land but also giving the land its famous 'Oregon Green' appearance.

As they drove the winding driveway into the property, the Mini had to pull over to allow a grain truck to squeeze past. The driver acknowledged the courtesy with a wave but seemed surprised that a cat was staring at him from its deluxe carrier next to the passenger window. Kate pulled into a space near the barns and prepared to cover her head with her hoodie.

Mum, please let me sit in here until the showers subside, whined Mo. *I don't particularly relish getting my fine fur wet.*

Although Kate wasn't entirely certain of the particular 'words' Mo had 'said,' she laughed because Mo, like most cats, dreaded going outside on the damp days. "I just don't see why you cats find a little shower so detestable. For goodness sake, you'd think that spitting on your paws and rubbing that spit onto your heads is so much more acceptable. Well, this little squall will last only a few minutes. I can see blue sky just there above the hills."

Mo wasn't to be dissuaded, so she rolled over, narrowed her eyes and planted her paws firmly on the carrier floor, letting her claws clamp down on the furry material like a vise. *Yes, mum, we'll just wait this out.*

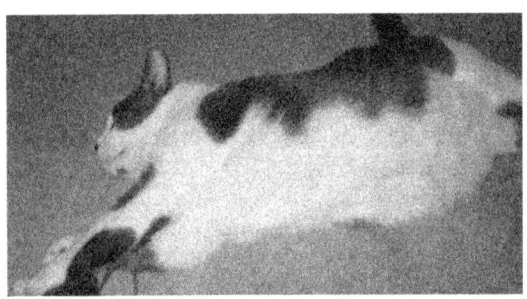

Always one to pick her battles, Kate decided to enjoy a favorite CD in the Mini's player, and settled in for the short wait. Sure enough, exactly five minutes later, the rain had stopped and the sun peeked out. "Look!" cried Kate. "There is the most beautiful rainbow over the hills, and perhaps if you'll let go of the fur in there, we might go look for the promised pot of gold."

Funny, mum. I don't like wet grass any better than I like a rain shower, but I suppose my paws could use a cooling off. Let's see if we can find Miss Lades and Señor in the barns. I think I see Olivia's father in the corral with a new colt. He appears to have his hands full!

CINCO DE MEOW

Chapter 4 –

The only thing more labor-intensive than catching a cat is catching two cats. One will go one way while the other will go the opposite way, as if by master plan. They take great pleasure in dividing our attention and multiplying our efforts. *Ryan Jeffrey Williams*

Kate opened the carrier and the car doors, and Mo jumped to the wet ground. Spotting four feline barn guards, Mo called to Lady, Señor, Winston and Squeaker, *Helloooooo! It's so good to see you!*

Lady turned her head and meowed to the two new arrivals – and nodded to acknowledge Winston and Squeaker, two inseparable and nearly-feral cats Olivia had recently adopted from Cats Pause as bonded companions and

19

mousing assistants for Lady and Señor in the barns.

Lady

Good morning Mo, mewed Lady. *We haven't had the pleasure of your company since we left the shelter. It's wonderful of you to visit us!*

CINCO DE MEOW

Squeaker and Winston

Mo meowed loudly in return. *Are you all doing any better now? I heard Olivia say you were up very early with the jitters. We've come to see if we can help you and the horses. What's up besides wet feet all around? I do so hate getting water on my lovely fur coat.*

I spied you tiptoeing through the gravel to avoid the grass, teased Lady. Squeaker and Winston in unison cried, *Woos!*

CINCO DE MEOW

Well, it has been a curious morning here, admitted Señor, *and I think Andrew Knightly is more than a little concerned that Donald hasn't arrived yet!*

Señor

What? Why do you think Donald didn't come to the barns today? I don't blame Mr. Knightly for being a little upset, cried Mo.

CINCO DE MEOW

Donald had also committed to helping with the new colt today, commented Winston. *Donald is younger and stronger than our Mr. Knightly, as is the colt, and it looks like the poor man is tiring with the stress of halter training already. The other horses have been snorting and whinnying with what feels like fear in the air.*

FEAR? queried Mo. *I don't doubt one bit that you and the horses are sensitive enough to detect that emotion when it exists. Could you determine if that fear emanated from human or animal or why the fear existed?*

It was so strong, we believe it was from a human – or humans, replied Squeaker. *But once the horses got wind of the scent, it was hard to tell. The air was just full of horse panic; and the poor colt was nearly sick with fright. I think that's why he's so hard to handle this morning.*

Kate caught up with Mo and approached the barn cautiously to avoid stepping in mud or onto a cat, having seen that the feline population here had increased somewhat.

The beautiful Tennessee Walkers were just finishing a late breakfast in their stalls, but the activity in the barn felt intense. The horses beat and scraped their hooves in the stalls, and they whinnied and neighed uncomfortably. Andrew Knightly was still out in the corral working with the new colt because, as they all now knew, Donald had not arrived this morning to take the reins.

Andrew was very obviously upset at Donald's absence, and was becoming weary with the energy of the colt. He thought of his daughter, Olivia, who was in her mid-twenties, loaded with energy and could easily handle the colt. Andrew was an 'older' parent, having waited to marry his Sara, now deceased, until he was in his early forties. He knew the joy of watching his daughter become the woman she was meant to be, a kind and gentle lady who worked because she loved any challenge, gave her time to others, and still tried to help her father on the ranch.

Olivia also volunteered at Cats Pause, and she had fostered, and then adopted the felines, Lady and Señor, and then Squeaker and Winston. She had a way with feral cats such as these. Those four cats had become more domesticated than they cared to admit, and they loved Olivia because she had earned their respect with kindness. Olivia returned the favour, and she also loved being around the cats and the horses at the ranch. The cats were ever mindful of the horses' hooves, but to their credit, the horses tolerated and respected the cats as well. It was a tit-for-tat relationship because the horses hated finding mice or their droppings in their food.

Kate noticed Andrew's apparent exhaustion, and she didn't want to upset the horses any further. While the cats seemed busily engaged with each other, she waved at Andrew, who waved back and then made his way toward her with the roped colt. The little guy was still too 'new' to wear a halter, but that would change with time and patience. He was beautiful, though, and tossed his small yet majestic head lightly with skittery confidence.

"Top of the mornin' to ye," shouted Andrew in his Scottish brogue. Andrew was a dual citizen, born in Scotland and raised in the USA. "Tis a wee hour for a visit from ye, but I'm more than glad to see ye!"

"Andrew, you really should wait for Donald to arrive. You've had your hands full feeding the horses and cleaning the stalls, and that colt is eyeing you like he's awaiting his chance to break away," admonished Kate.

"There now Kate," replied Andrew, "what meld of rancher would I be if I couldn't control me' own colt? He's a feisty wee thing, but he loves to nuzzle and that's a good sign. I'm just a mite preoccupied with worry about Donald. He has never, I say never, failed to call if he's been waylaid or ill. Heaven forbid and I hope he's not injured - and he'd not miss his opportunities at the ranch for anything short of dire injury or illness. Why, the horses are practically wild this morning without hearing his voice. He soothes them. They're used to him and they miss him. Aye, I'll never get them calmed down."

CINCO DE MEOW

Chapter 5 –

What greater gift than the love of a cat? *Charles Dickens*

Andrew put the colt in his stall and gave him fresh hay. He and Kate started to gather the cats to go inside, when Andrew stopped short.

"Look, over there, behind the tractor storage barn," shouted Andrew, "that's Donald's pickup!"

"Good grief," exclaimed Kate. "It's parked just out of sight from the main barn and no wonder we missed it. Let's go check the truck and see if the keys are in there, or perhaps we'll find that Donald simply fell asleep behind the wheel."

As they approached the truck, cats and humans walking single file, all five cats started hissing and arching their backs, their tails bottle-brushed and their fur standing straight up like broom bristles.

"Oh oh," grimaced Kate. "The cats are sensing something strange – or sinister. Maybe we should stay back from the truck so we don't trample the ground, muck up the area or let the cats get any more agitated."

"Aye, that's a fair point, Kate," said Andrew. "I can walk carefully to the driver's door. I dunna' recommend going together, just in case there *is* something on the ground or around the truck that needs preserving."

Andrew treading softly reached the door and peered inside. "He's not in the truck and I admit to being glad for that," cried Andrew. "I had awful things going 'round in me' head about that. The doors are locked and I dunna' see the keys on the seat or around the console."

Andrew then carefully approached the passenger door and started to reach for the door handle. He thought better of it and shielded his eyes to look inside. "I dunna' see anything unusual on the front seats, either. I suppose he might have gone home last evening with a friend or perhaps the truck was having mechanical problems. But why wouldn't he call me to let me know?

"Something's not right and I canna' just stand here and do nothing. I was going to the pasture to check out the horses anyway. Kate, ye'd be better off waiting here while I investigate."

"I'm worried, too, Andrew," said Kate. "I want to go with you. Let me don my galoshes so my feet at least stay dry. They're on the floor of the Mini's back seat."

Although the rain was now punishing, Andrew, Kate with galoshes and the cats (all the while in constant protest to the rain) started out around the barns, past the corral and out into the pasture. They were too worried to let the rain stop them. The cats squealed and tiptoed but were soon soaked and muddy, as their trek took them far into the field.

But suddenly, the wet day seemed the least of their worries. Cat and human alike stood stock still. There on the ground, not fifty feet from their location lay Donald!

"Oh nooooo," cried Kate. "Poor Donald! There's so much blood! Andrew, please go and check for vital signs, and I'll try to hold reign on the cats. They look terrified!"

Andrew, as carefully as possible, waded in the mud to Donald, and put his finger on Donald's throat seeking a pulse. There was none.

"Kate, I know ye always have yer phone with ye. Please call Lieutenant Charles Beltz of the McMinnville Police. There's nothing we can do for Donald. He's gone!"

CINCO DE MEOW

Chapter 6 –

Cats do care. For example they know instinctively what time we have to be at work in the morning and they wake us up twenty minutes before the alarm goes off. *Michael Nelson*

Kate was in a state of shock as she made her way to the shelter with Mo. Olivia and Victoria would be in fine charge at the shelter, and Kate was not the least concerned that they could handle the numbers of cats and the visitors today. Certainly, by the time Kate arrived they had completed the cleaning chores and the shelter looked spic and span. Kate knew, because she had been a volunteer at the shelter before she became its director, that the pay received by the volunteers, in the form of head butts, paw taps and purrs, was far and away better compensation than money. What she didn't know was how to tell Olivia about Donald.

Once inside, Kate gently pulled Olivia aside into her office, and put her arms around the young lady. "Olivia," Kate spoke softly, "I have some very bad news. There's no way to soften this blow, so I'll just tell you that your beloved friend, Donald, was found lifeless this morning at the ranch."

Olivia stood absolutely stock still and held her breath. "I can't believe it! I saw Donald late yesterday, and he was going to help da' with the colt today! What happened? It just can't be true!"

"Olivia," said Kate, "your father is there at the ranch, and I'm sure you'll want to go to him now. The shelter will be fine today as I've called in two more volunteers, Rebecca Sherlock and Elizabeth Conley, who are more than willing to share some duties with Victoria. I think Andrew needs you more than we do, and at least as much as you need him. I don't know all the details but I know your place is by his side."

CINCO DE MEOW

In a daze, Olivia grabbed her coat and left the shelter. She needed her father so much and she couldn't believe Donald was dead!

Kate waited for Elizabeth and Rebecca to arrive. Elizabeth was a good friend who had fostered and then adopted Phillip, a beautiful Maine Coon cat (with only one seeing eye) from the shelter. Although she had her hands full with her Print Shoppe business, she gladly helped out at the shelter when she could. Rebecca had lost her husband, Lawrence in the past year to a heinous murder. But then she gave birth to Lawrence, Jr. and adopted the lovely black cat and Mo's best friend, Georgia, to rebuild her family. She, too, gave of her time at the shelter when needed because she so admired the good work the shelter was doing for the community.

Having given no further information about Donald to the two volunteers, Kate felt a bit guilty. But then, she didn't want to adulterate the pending murder investigation with innuendo and gossip. So she waded again through the puddles back to her car. Mo stayed behind at the shelter to explain the morning's events to the cats, and to try and settle everyone down.

CINCO DE MEOW

Kate drove on to the winery where she needed to resume her duties as the Cinco de Mayo event coordinator. Mostly, though, she wanted to be busy and useful – and push the picture of Donald's lifeless body out of her mind. Kate loved the shelter, she loved being with the cats and couldn't get enough of the human generosity she witnessed each day at the site. Certainly more humanity than some lowly miscreant had shown to Donald.

But there were also a few shelter update articles and adoption notices she wanted to post online for the shelter bulletin, *Pause for the Claws*. They were mostly completely written and edited, and she could post them along with photos later.

She did want to focus on finishing the Cinco de Mayo Event 'serving phase,' though, and it was good to keep her mind focused on things other than the mental picture of Donald's violent death. Kate knew that the investigation was in good hands with Lieutenant Charles Beltz, so she busied herself as best she could until she could be of more assistance if needed.

Shortly after arriving at the winery, Kate gently informed Mary about Donald. Mary hadn't known Donald well, but she was an extremely compassionate person and knew how much he would be missed, not only by his human friends, but by the animals he so lovingly cared for.

Kate decided to call Charles, her friend and confidant, who happened to be 'The Law' in the Seven Oaks area. Charles had attended Linfield College and Western Oregon University where he majored in law enforcement. Charles particularly liked his position as the Yamhill County liaison between community and law enforcement. It gave him an opportunity to find out what people in the community liked, disliked and most of all needed from law enforcement, and on the other hand, he put the skills in law enforcement he mastered so well into practice to uphold that law in this small community. He was also liaison between city police, county sheriffs and the state police, and worked to share communications between those groups, making them stronger and more consistent in their practices.

Charles' working office was located in McMinnville, where he owned a very nice cottage of his own to return to at the end of the day. Charles had recently published a cookbook entitled, *The Compleat Jory Hills Wine Country*

Cuisine/Wine Pairing Journal. He had taken much teasing from friends and at the department with the announcement of that book, although nowhere is it written that a police officer cannot be a chef or an author, for that matter.

Charles and Kate had become much more than friends now that they had chosen to tell each how the other felt. Charles loved Kate, and to his utter amazement, she loved him back! Charles had even dubbed in his book a particularly savoury pairing of pinot noir and rib eye steak, 'Kate's Dinner Choice.' Kate still felt shy about her feelings for Charles, but they were both beginning to understand that what passed between them was more meaningful than they had previously imagined. Each had been so busy building careers and staunching old wounds, it was a relief to both to have someone to confide in, and most of all, to respect and depend upon.

Charles was very glad to hear from Kate, but the conversation was somewhat stinted because Charles was only beginning the new investigation into Donald's death, and he couldn't share many details at this point with Kate. Not that this early in the investigation there were many details at all in the case. Just speaking with him, though, made Kate feel better, and she hung up the phone with a smile knowing she would see him later that day.

Chapter 7 –

The reason cats climb is so that they can look down on almost every other animal…it's also the reason they hate birds. *KC Buffington*

To alleviate the tension at the winery, Mary and Kate thought it best to move the subject away from murder. So they set about discussing wines and marketing, namely a change in the way wines would be sold that would have an effect on the upcoming event.

To accommodate this change, they'd need not only wine glasses both with stems and without, but because of new possibilities with respect to wine packaging, John had ordered special Kats Jory Hills Estate Growlers in several styles to sell – and to fill – at the event.

The Oregon legislature had passed a bill that would allow wine to be sold in large, customer-supplied containers or "growlers." This meant that Oregon wine drinkers could now bring their favorite pinot noir, cabernet or pinot gris home in bulk by the growler – as beer aficionados had been doing for years. The bill was an important concept that would help the wine industry expand its customer base, as well as create more environmentally sustainable customer service. It allowed wine and cider to be sold in up to two-gallon containers that could be cleaned and reused.

However, the federal Alcohol and Tobacco Tax and Trade Bureau issued a ruling that pronounced selling wine in refillable containers was illegal unless a business had a bottling license. In the end, U. S. Senator, Ron Wyden complained to the federal agency, which finally backed off and issued its final verdict saying growlers for wine were OK.

A few wineries had already partnered with restaurants to sell their wines from stainless steel *casks* after the development of an argon gas-enabled dispensing system that wouldn't interfere with a wine's particular taste. Those wineries especially, were heralding the introduction of the growler to the Oregon wine consumer.

Now Oregon was coming in line with the rest of the wine industry, but also stepping respectfully ahead in several respects. Oregon's growlers wouldn't be just any old jug. They would become highly sophisticated containers that could have their own argon dispensing system intact in them. Oregon would be the first state in the nation to allow growler fill-ups at wineries. This new packaging had many benefits to growers, bottlers and the community as a whole.

Winemakers knew that allowing refillable wine growlers would help the industry expand their markets, become more environmentally friendly and boost sales. Wine could become more normal and a part of everyday moderate consumption. In 2011, the state's 463 wineries raked in about $2.7 billion, selling more than 2 million cases of wine. By 2015, there were 676 wineries in Oregon. Without the cost of packaging and labeling a bottle, restaurants and consumers could save money from purchasing wine in bulk. The price of wine by the keg or growler would cost just half the retail price of buying the same quantity by the bottle.

While it might seem odd to pour wine out of a keg, consumers had already liked it that way more than they knew. Many restaurants had switched to kegs to fill wine by the glass and cut costs. One keg replaced 39 bottles. A whole lot of energy was used to melt down the bottles and remake them, both in the heat and the transportation. Winemakers had to secure corks, labels and the bottles. All of that effort as well as the tangible product was energy intensive.

Although some might say that people would not adjust to large volume wine packaging because they still liked the romance of pulling the cork out, fine wines would likely not be packaged thus. No one was expecting to see anyone walking down the street with a gallon growler of a fine Estate Reserve Pinot Noir. But they would hopefully choose to purchase in bulk the lesser-to medium-priced wines, like a good red or white blend or a mild chardonnay or pinot gris via the growler.

So Kats Jory Hills Estate Winery would offer reusable growlers for sale. Those growlers would display the Kats' winery logo and would be top-of-the-line technologically and ecologically.

Kate and Mary were proud to be a part of the cutting edge in wine dispensing at the winery.

But the air still needed further clearing and Mary was feeling, rightfully so, helpless in that there was little she could do for Kate. So she broached the topic of Kate's new bed-and-breakfast venture. Although she knew Kate had opened for business the month before, Mary merely had to ask Kate how the B&B project was coming along to get Kate to open up – wide.

"Well, Mary, thank you for asking!" exclaimed Kate. "I'm so grateful to have completed my long-awaited bed-and-breakfast establishment. When I first laid eyes on the carriage house at father's vineyard and farm, I gave the idea of developing a B&B or guest house serious thought. But there were so many other things to do. As you know, I take my duties as director of Cats Pause very seriously.

"And I also needed to give my dad much support during the terrible time he had fought with the local licensing bureau to complete his winery and open the tasting room.

"After resolution of that mess, I was doubly glad that I would not have to worry about the kind of licensing nightmare for the B&B that my father had experienced in building the tasting room."

That licensing and coding process was cleaned up when Kate's father, John, and his winemaker, William Kent, along with Charles and the FBI – assisted by Mo, of course – broke up a plot to hinder local wineries from interstate wine sales by crippling the facilities from which the wine was produced and marketed. A group of California wholesalers had attempted to do so by sabotaging the facilities' equipment and planting bogus licensing inspectors who would then deny applications for winery improvement or operation. There were also a few 'bad apples' in the licensing bureau itself that were culled out as a result of this effort.

Once John's winery and tasting room began operating successfully, Kate knew she could make the time to turn her dream of being a wine country hostess into a reality. Bolstered by some of Mary's wonderful ideas, Kate enlisted the help of several local carpenters, contractors and architects, who worked to expand the carriage house to accommodate up to six couples in tastefully apportioned rooms. Kate's own quarters were at the back of the establishment, with fabulous views of the vineyards and the Oregon Coast Range.

"I've added six full baths to the suites in the carriage house, as well, and it's the only B&B in the area that can boast private loos for each suite. You may remember that I made the decision, although an expensive investment, after you shared a horrific 'adventure' you'd experienced at a B&B at the Oregon beach!"

Several years prior, there had been five "couples" staying at a Nye Beach B&B, which featured only two full baths for the entire establishment. That meant trips down the hall requiring full dress or at least full coverage; inconvenient in the middle of the night and downright chilly after a shower or bath. The coast B&B had also served breakfast from seven to nine in the morning and tea at three in the afternoon. Since the two repasts were included in the price of the rooms, everyone made certain to partake in both to secure their money's worth. Unfortunately, one of the food items served on a particular day had contained something akin to the Noro-Virus, rendering those who had previously enjoyed the delicious but tainted food, with severe stomach and intestinal cramps.

Mary Malone, who had been at the B&B paired with her sister Victoria, had become gravely ill, and the lack of privacy in the loo was devastating. Two members of the guest parties had actually been taken to the hospital. After that, Mary had vowed never to seek accommodation without a private loo – and to be especially careful what she ate at any B&B. It did pay to examine the rating of the host, caterer or restaurant before you ate their cuisine. When she had revealed the story to Kate, it was instantly clear to Kate that most people would probably prefer the privacy of the full bath in their suite, so Kate requested the necessary architectural designs.

"Even after hearing of the debacle at the coast, I wanted to serve breakfast and tea at the B&B. In any case, you know I always rise very early and never miss breakfast, so why not share the wealth? So I prepare a hearty English breakfast for my guests, as well, or they can choose a lighter fare featuring fresh fruit in season, biscuits and oatmeal. It took me some time to name the new establishment, but I settled on father's idea, Kats English Bed and Breakfast."

Mary would sometimes stop by the B&B on her way to the clinic to chat with the guests, and to offer suggestions for wine tours and fine dining. She sometimes helped out by washing up any leftover baking or dining dishes, but Kate by that time had already made the beds and cleaned the six new bathrooms before heading off to Cats Pause. Kate's father, John would also stop by to make sure the guests were in need of naught. Since his house was conveniently located on the property with the B&B, he was always close by if needed. And he relished the opportunity to speak with people from other areas or countries because not only did he have so much local knowledge to offer, he in turn learned much about visitors' wine and food choices, which provided immeasurable insight for his business.

Kate would return to the B&B in mid-afternoon to prepare tea. She loved to bake the scones and serve them warm with real cream. Because she made the experience so pleasant, she found few weekends when suites were still available to let, especially if a wine tasting event was occurring in the area.

Now Kate and Mary finished their tasks aided by their discussions. But the strain of the day had left them both quite drained. Mary wanted to stop by the shelter to help close up and see if any new kitties had arrived. Kate would go to the B&B for afternoon tea, then she would also stop by Cats Pause to see if Mo wanted to come home and sleep in her own bed, or if the feline ambassador would rather stay with a new arrival at the shelter, comforting and supporting the little orphan, and promising to help find him or her a loving home.

Chapter 8 –

A cat can maintain a position of curled up somnolence on your knee until you are nearly upright. To the last minute she hopes your conscience will get the better of you and you will settle down again. *Pam Brown*

James Middleton lingered at the Cats Pause Shelter hoping to see Mary, but he was also happy to see the cats and Victoria, as well as Rebecca and Elizabeth when they arrived. Since he had more time there, he'd make sure there were no new arrivals that needed his attention. He brought with him for a visit his two adopted cats, Andrew and Sarah, nicknamed for the wine county area, Arbor and Syrah.

James had gone to college in Corvallis, and had been a talented baseball player. He had not taken his studies seriously because he loved the game so much. He had also loved the ladies so much. James became known as an adept player, both on and off the field. He'd become friends with Kate through her then-fiancé, Brian, but their friendship was centered on their collective love of baseball. Brian was staunchly loyal to Kate, and wouldn't have dreamed of fooling around on her. Sadly, Brian was later killed in service to his country, which left Kate with shattered dreams and James with the loss of his best friend.

But then James met Sally, and he decided he'd had enough games. He enrolled in OSU's School of Veterinary Medicine, and he and Sally were married within three months. James loved Sally, but he became so obsessed with animal medicine that he began paying less and less attention to her. Sally had been a cheerleader in college, and she wasn't used to being ignored. She soon became bored and sought attention with other suitors. James' marriage ended as it had begun: in a flash.

CINCO DE MEOW

James was devastated by the loss of Sally, but he took solace in his veterinarian duties and his love of animals. He eventually moved to Seven Oaks, opened his own clinic, the Cats Meow, and volunteered as veterinarian at Cats Pause Shelter. There he met Mary Malone, and when she applied for a position as his assistant at the clinic, he hired her immediately.

Because Mary and Kate were so close and the two shared interests in viticulture and wines, James began to learn much about the vineyards by spending time with them. In collaboration with Kate's father John, and his winemaker William, James helped introduce the first Governor's Wine Cellar in Oregon. The "Wine and Vine," which was a collection of the state's best wines, was to be used for state dinners and entertaining. Washington State followed that lead, so that both states boasted fine wines at the Governor's Mansion. The Governor's Wine Cellar brought much attention both nationally and internationally to Oregon's wines, and introduced a variety of local pinot noirs into new markets. This provided exposure for many smaller wineries, including Kats Jory Hills Estate Winery.

CINCO DE MEOW

The state of Colorado boasted a governor's beer cellar. Although Oregon was also becoming a craft beer empire, the wine industry leaders had gotten in ahead to establish the wine cellar in the state house!

Mo spotted Arbor and Syrah as they waited patiently in the lobby.

Good morning my friends, Mo meowed in greeting. *I'm so happy to see you. Did you hear about Donald's murder?*

Yes, shocking! cried Arbor and Syrah in unison.

Donald was such a kind man and so good with animals, lamented Syrah as she rubbed against Mo. *Why, when James visited the Knightly Ranch to tend to the horses' medical needs, Donald would always come looking for us with treats, and he would call Lady and Señor to come and see us. As soon as Winston and Squeaker became part of the ranch family, he would look for them, too, to make sure we all got to socialize. What a dreadful thing to happen and we will miss him so!*

I was actually present when Donald's body was found, Mo shared with the two friends. *It was certainly no accident. There was* blood all over the poor man. I listened to Mum and Andrew talking before they called the police, and they concluded Donald must have been killed, and most likely with a knife.

Ugh, cried Arbor in disgust. *Humans can be so vile. We only kill to eat and to keep creatures like rodents from overpopulating areas where they interfere with human activities. Have you any idea who would want to kill Donald?*

No, not at all, Mo confessed, *but Donald, nice as he was, wasn't much into the whole vineyard scene, even though the ranch has a small vineyard. He loved animals and he loved the Knightly Ranch and its occupants. The only thing I ever heard about Donald outside of his life at the ranch was his recent interest in the Newberg-Seven Oaks-Dundee Bypass. He told Kate just a few days ago that he had some information that would help move the project along, and he hoped the opposing factions didn't get ahold of the information before he could present it to the county commissioners. He felt those factions had been known to wage negative campaigns when things didn't go their way. He also felt the bypass would be good for* all the vineyards and certainly for all the businesses in the area.

Well, mewed Syrah, *the information Donald was keeping secret just might have been his downfall. Secrets! Why do humans insist on being so secretive about everything? With a cat (if we so choose), you will know if we're pleased or displeased, you can tell anything by looking at our faces. A human can hide feelings all day. I wonder what information Donald had that was such a big secret? Could it have been damaging enough to the opposition to invite a death sentence? I mean really: a stupid road? Well, humans do love their cars and they get very upset when bad drivers and bad roads slow them down.*

The cats would speculate for the next ten minutes about the "big secret," until James called Syrah and Arbor for their departure. They vowed to keep their ears open to their humans' discussions about Donald and to listen for any clues that might help them solve the mystery of his death. After all, who wants a killer loose on the streets of Seven Oaks?

CINCO DE MEOW

Chapter 9 –

Our perfect companions never have fewer than four feet.
Colette

Many Yamhill County residents had waited a lifetime to see work begin on the Newberg-Seven Oaks-Dundee bypass. County Commissioner, George King, could relate. "It was certainly one of the issues I campaigned on in 1994 when I first ran for Commissioner. It's been my political lifelong dream to get this project done."

George saw firsthand the need for such a project when he and his wife operated a business in downtown Seven Oaks. Every day outside the building, congested traffic on

Oregon Route 99W would fill the air with exhaust and generate enough noise to rattle windows. Plus, pedestrian crossings were unsafe.

For decades, traffic problems had plagued Highway 99W, which passes through downtowns Newberg, Dundee and Seven Oaks. Multiple bypass proposals were presented, but money always seemed to be a roadblock. That changed in 2001, when the Legislature provided the Oregon Department of Transportation a $190 million grant to start the first phase of a $760.6 million project.

Now, after almost a decade of planning, ground was scheduled to broken sometime in August.

"I can take a great sigh of relief of accomplishment at this point," said George. "I've been involved in this as long as I've been a commissioner...it's going to give us a new breath of life."

The project called for creation of an eleven-mile route along the outskirts of Newberg, Dundee and Seven Oaks and near to McMinnville, Dayton and Lafayette. Traffic was expected to decrease by as much as sixty percent in some places after the bypass opened.

The high cost ($257 million) of just the first phase was tied to the expensive properties that ODOT would need to buy around Newberg, where the highway would begin. Other phases would not require such expensive property acquisition.

"The project is expected to improve accessibility and free up parking spaces for people who patronize downtown Newberg, Dundee and Seven Oaks businesses," said George. "It also will help attract new businesses. Businesses look at that traffic and say, 'I don't want to locate my shop where we're going to have to deal with this severe bottleneck every single day.' It's an economic necessity for our county."

Additionally, the project would reduce the amount of "through traffic," which accounts for ninety percent of the total in towns like Seven Oaks. For George, it also meant that his kitties, Mona, Mac and Murphy, would experience less noise and stress as they approached mature age. George doted on the cats, so he and his wife were even more pleased that they could look forward to opening their windows in summer without the roar of log trucks zooming by and scaring the cats.

"It's been a long, long time, but we're delighted it has come this far, and we're ready to see it move ahead," George said. "Even so, work on only the first phase is not expected to be finished until 2016."

The promise of a new bypass made most people quite happy.

But not everyone, it appeared, was pleased with traffic being diverted from their front doors.

Chapter 10 –

A cat can purr its way out of anything. *Donna McCrohan*

Kate was glad to be back at the B&B. Most of her guests had gone out for dinner, taking advantage of the many delicious offerings of cuisine in the area's local restaurants. She'd prepared the basics for tomorrow's breakfast, and set the tables for her ten guests' morning pleasure.

Now she sat in her suite before the fire with a glass of fine Kats Jory Hills Estate Pinot Noir. What a horrible day it had been.

Her cell phone rang. She looked at the digital display and was thrilled to see that it was Charles calling her.

CINCO DE MEOW

"Hello Charles," cooed Kate when she spoke into her iPhone. "I've been hoping you'd call. This day has been absolutely dreadful and I let Mo stay at the shelter because there were two new arrivals. It's so quiet here without her. Sometimes I can't believe she's a cat. She keeps me company much in the way a human would."

"Hmmm," mused Charles. "I hope Mo doesn't keep such good company that you'll not want anyone else to be around. I might begin to take offense at playing second fiddle to a cat, even if the cat is as smart as Mo."

Kate laughed. "Now Charles, you know that Mo is special to me, but she doesn't take me for dinner or hold my hand or read aloud to me when my eyes hurt. Nor does she cook up such wonderful recipes in the kitchen, and you know she hates the movies, not to mention the opera and the ballet!"

"Well, I guess I'm safe in your affections then," laughed Charles. "Would you by chance mind some company tonight? I have a situation I'd like to discuss with you. I can't tell you very much about the status of the case itself as it's about Donald's death, but there are a few things I'd like to run by your creative mind. You always see things I don't."

"I'll look forward to seeing you," replied Kate.

Twenty minutes later, Charles drove into the covered portico of the coach house B&B. He was thinking how proud he was of Kate for starting this business. This, on top of her duties at the shelter and helping her father in the vineyard and winery, surprised him that she made any time for him at all. But he was glad she did!

Kate opened her side-entrance French doors to greet Charles. He always chose this entrance as it was convenient to the driveway at the rear of the B&B, and guests would not be using it. He stood gazing at Kate for a few seconds, then took her in his arms and kissed her. They had arrived at the stage in their relationship where a kiss in greeting was not only acceptable, but something to look forward to.

"My goodness, Kate," Charles admonished, "you look ghastly! I suppose that remark will set me down a notch or two in your 'favorite' rankings, but it's quite obvious you are distraught over the events of today. Let's have a spot of tea, if you don't mind."

CINCO DE MEOW

"Aaahh, Charles," Kate sighed, "I take no offense because I look like I feel: dreadful. I simply can't get used to seeing death in its violent, unnatural form, and it seems I've seen quite a few. Tea sounds wonderful. I'll just set the kettle on. Milk then?"

"Please," replied Charles. "While you're tending tea, I'll give you a brief summary. Most of what I'll be telling you will be in the *Jory Hill Times* tomorrow. George King was, of course, quick to the scene, not only because he is editor of the *Times*, but as Yamhill County Commissioner, he was required to sign off on some of the paperwork for the force. I'll begin with the basics."

"Just a moment, Charles," begged Kate. "I'd like to sit down and have my biscuits warmed before you begin."

When the tea and biscuits were prepared, Charles carried the tray down the hall to the parlour, and they settled in on the sofa, side-by-side.

"Well, Kate," began Charles, "you were there when Andrew found Donald's body, so you know the basics. Donald was stabbed several times in the chest, and he died of exsanguination, or blood loss. Now, use of a knife by a perpetrator usually means the crime was personal. Whomever did this stood face-to-face with Donald when the first blow was struck. We don't have a murder weapon, however, so the killer must have taken it with him.

"The medical examiner believes the murder occurred at about five o'clock this morning. Since the crime occurred on a working ranch with pretty set hours for livestock feeding, it's possible that someone saw the perpetrator around that time. Now there were footprints leading out to where Donald was found, and we've eliminated Andrew's and Donald's. The rain blurred them a bit, but still, there are at least five different sets out there."

"I was fairly close, as well, Charles," admitted Kate. "Do you need the galoshes I wore this morning for comparison?"

"Yes, please Kate," said Charles. "That will eliminate one more set, which leaves two sets of footprints to investigate. It also appears that Donald was killed where he fell because there were no blood trails. We did find several drops of blood close by, but that could indicate that the killer or killers had blood contact, that the knife was still dripping blood or that Donald was able to do some damage to his killer before he died. We'll know about the blood donor when we get the lab results back. In any case, the location of the blood drops gives us at least an indication of which direction the killer went after he killed Donald. After the stabbing, it appears that the perpetrator ran from the pasture around the equipment barn and into the vineyard, most likely because the vines provided fair shelter from anyone who happened to be coming out to the barns."

"Hmm. Interesting. I'll run get those galoshes," said Kate. "I've cleaned them up pretty well, so I hope you weren't counting on any samples from them."

"No ma'am," replied Charles. "Any samples we might need will come from Andrew's work boots because he didn't get a chance to clean his shoes. I'd sure like to stay longer this evening, Kate, but I must get the boots back to the office and to the lab, and I have several leads I still need to follow up before the trail gets too cold."

"Of course," replied Kate in return. "I'm just exhausted anyway, and I fear, not very good company."

Kate left the parlour and returned shortly with the boots she had worn that morning at the ranch. She held a reusable plastic grocery bag to place them in for transport. "Here they are. I'll be glad when I'm eliminated from suspicion, so please let me know when that happens, Charles."

"I certainly will do that," said Charles. "Of course, there would never be any reason to suspect you of this deed. But I do understand you'd like to be canceled from a list of possible suspects with haste. Don't worry, Kate, just get some rest and I'll come by to see you in the morning. Now, may I please kiss you goodnight? That will keep me warm on the drive back to the department."

"Oh, Charles," sighed Kate. "You do not have to ask anymore, you know. I so enjoy your company and a goodnight kiss will warm me as well while I prepare for bed."

After Charles left, Kate sat on the sofa with her knees pulled up to her chin. What a wonderful friend Charles had become, she thought. And I do so love the taste of his lips and the wonderful masculine scent of his aftershave. I don't know what I've done to garner his trust and friendship, but I'm glad he feels the same way about me as I do about him!

Chapter 11 –

A dog will look at you with adoration and devotion in his eyes; but as the Egyptians discovered, you must worship the cat. *Olivia Williams Rial*

The morning dawned crisp and clear. Yesterday's showers had passed, and the flowers and grasses were perked up and happy in the face of the sun.

Mo had spent the night at the shelter where she tutored two kittens in the ways of being charming, alert, box-trained and adoptable.

She was just returning to Kate's office for a nap when she heard her wonderful friend,

CINCO DE MEOW

Georgia, in the lobby. Georgia kept her human, Rebecca Sherlock, good company. Rebecca had adopted Georgia from Cats Pause after her late husband Lawrence, who had been the night custodian at the shelter, had been murdered. Rebecca and Georgia were delighted to welcome Lawrence, Jr. to their family, and the three were like peas in a pod. Sure enough, Lawrence, Jr. or Junior as they called him, was sleeping soundly in his carriage with all the noise in the lobby going unnoticed.

"Mo!" exclaimed Rebecca. "We've missed you so. It must be a month since we've seen you. What with Junior's doctor appointments and my exercising to lose baby weight, I've been quite busy. Not to mention my new reunion business, 'Let's Get Together' has taken off much faster than I had expected. I'm so sorry we've not visited you more often!"

Mo purred her pleasure at seeing the group, and rubbed along Rebecca's leg for good measure.

Georgia, I've missed you so! We must find a way for us to get together when our humans are too busy to transport us!

Agreed, mewed Georgia, who rubbed Mo's head with her own. *Rebecca insisted on stopping by the shelter to offer her condolences to Olivia. She said there was so much confusion yesterday, and Olivia had gone to the ranch by the time Rebecca finished helping the cats and volunteers get organized. I know Olivia adored Donald. I didn't know him well, but I had met him on several occasions. He was always respectful of cats.*

Georgia

Mum says Charles stopped by last night to see her, said Mo. *You do know that Mum and I were at the ranch when Donald was found. She's just had a beastly few days. I was with Lady, Señor, Winston and Squeaker at the ranch. We stayed well away from poor Donald as there was so much blood. It made my normally sleek hair stand straight up. We all were just terrified. And the horses were nearly catatonic with fear. The unrest also prompted the new colt to give Andrew a very bad time in the arena. These are strange times, and the animals all feel the changes.*

What have you heard from Kate, Mo? asked Georgia. *My mum says the newspaper had a very thorough write-up about Donald's murder, if that's what it was.*

Well, hissed Mo, *for starters, the police don't appear to have a motive for murder, so they don't know that it was murder. But you know, Donald told Kate he had information about that new highway bypass that he was anxious to share with the commissioners. He said it was important, and that he hoped the opposition didn't find out about it until he'd had a chance to present his findings to the commission. You know, secrets are a terrible thing. Secrecy never really helps anybody! It also appears to be the only lead on a motive we can find. I'm going to start digging out just who might have a stake in keeping the highway through-traffic at status quo, and I know just who to ask! I think we need to pay a visit to George King, and Mona, Mac and Murphy. They're in the best positions to give us information on anything having to do with the county and its blasted roads!*

CINCO DE MEOW

Chapter 12 –

If the pull of the outside world is strong for a cat, there is also a pull towards the human. The cat may disappear on its own errands, but sooner or later, it returns once again for a little while, to greet us with its own type of love.
Independent as they are, cats find more than pleasure in our company. *Lloyd Alexander*

Spring was a Kitten Calamity everywhere. People who didn't spay or neuter their pets found themselves with unwanted kittens and puppies at this time of year. For ferals and strays, unless someone who knew the ins and outs of trapping the females – and also the males – for neutering, or some charitable organization found them (think Feral Cat

Coalition), kittens were born to feral moms who did their best to feed and care for them, sometimes at the cost of the feral mom's life. Some fared better than others, depending on the human or humans with whom they were associated, or whether they were linked to any humans at all.

The Spay Station, Dr. James Middleton's mobile veterinary clinic, worked in tandem with several agencies to try and save and place these kittens. Mona, Mac and Murphy had been one of James' feral family success stories.

Mona, a feral tiger-striped female, had mated several years before with a Maine Coon male somewhere around the Seven Oaks area. By the time Mona was able to leave her new kittens to look for food, they were all nearly starved.

Luckily, James found Mona around the back steps of his home, where he sometimes left food out for cats this time of year with the trap-neuter-release purpose in mind. Mona, though wild, was lured by James' soft tenor voice, and she came back day after day at the same time, around four in the afternoon for scraps and milk to eat so she could produce milk for her kittens. James became attached to the pretty little tiger cat, and he would watch for her. James never left food out when he wasn't home, because the raccoons, bobcats and coyotes were also attracted to the cat food. James' house became part of Mona's daily routine in her quest for food.

One day, after about a month of these clandestine encounters, Mona brought with her two little kittens. Mona and her babies sat patiently outside James' back door (she had progressed to the porch in her daily search for food). James opened the door cautiously and the cats backed up, ready to run. He spoke very softly to them and moved with precise caution to leave some canned cat food and two small bowls of milk for the group. He slowly backed inside and gently closed the door. But he so enjoyed watching them from his vantage point in the window at the top of the door.

One warm, sunny day, as summer was approaching, he left the back door open. He placed food on the porch, but also in the mud room inside. The cats finished the small portion of food on the porch and then slowly ventured inside where other nutritious treats awaited.

And so this routine continued for nearly a week. At the end of that time, James would sit on the floor and wait for the cats to enter. One day, at the end of the second week, both kittens sidled up to James and rubbed their tiny heads on his slacks. James was hesitant to touch them back, so he waited until their next visit. On that encounter, the kittens again approached James and rubbed against his legs. One of them curled up with his back to the warm leg he had found: that was Mac. Murphy on the other hand, though curious and also wishing for a warm area to nap, wandered back to Mona, who stood licking her paws in the doorway.

This slow acquainting went on for the next month, and by the end of that month, all three cats would allow James to close the back door for short periods while they investigated the house. They always came back to the door and stood there patiently for James to allow them back outside.

One day, George King came to visit James at his home, and just happened to be there when the three cats came to call. George was immediately smitten, but James knew he couldn't attempt to move the cats at this stage. George returned day after day, though, so the cats soon came to know him as well as they knew James. George brought fresh ground meat and cream and soon the cats would allow him to touch them lightly. When the kittens were old enough, now several months, George and James put food inside a cozy cage, with a spring loaded door. As soon as all three cats were inside, the door shut. Of course, this was not received well by the cats, and they hissed and snapped, finally settling down to eat their dinners.

When their tummies were satisfied, James took them to the Spay Station, where he notched their ears, administered their vaccinations and relieved them of their reproductive organs. It took the cats several days to recover, and later, James took the cats to George's house, where George and his wife had readied an indoor home for the group. It took the cats several weeks of hiding under the bed in the room to which they were confined to trust George again. James also came to visit to make sure they had healed and that they were not injuring themselves trying to get out. At the end of that time, though, the cats seemed to enjoy the protection and serenity of their indoor setting, and began adjusting to their new home.

CINCO DE MEOW

Mona

Mac

CINCO DE MEOW

Murphy

Now, Mona, Mac and Murphy viewed the approach of Georgia and Morgan from their respective perches in George's front windows. Spying each other, the cats became excited with anticipation of the impending visit.

Morgan! Georgia! screeched Mona from her pillowed perch. *It's been ages! We heard George speaking with Kate, so we knew Kate was going to drop you both off for a visit while she and Rebecca go for coffee.*

CINCO DE MEOW

Boy, mewed Georgia, *we had to do some major whining and flipping onto our backs and dancing — to get those two to let us go for a ride. It just so happened that Kate spoke with George just as we were leaving Cats Pause, and George invited us for a visit. Wow, you three have really redecorated the place!*

The cats were all viewing George's front windows and his front porch, which had been "massaged" to become cat-friendly. The windows were now sans blinds and curtains, and hummingbird feeders hung safely outside for the enjoyment of both bird and feline. The front porch had five chairs lined up behind the railing: two human-sized Adirondack chairs book-ended three small Adirondack chairs, each with its own pillow bearing the particular cat's name to which it belonged. The cats already had their favorite chairs on which their respective named pillows were place, but it amazed George and his wife that they always, always jumped into the chair bearing the pillow with their own names.

Yes, it does take some time to communicate with humans, Mac replied, *but we think we did a jolly good job on this aspect. On our chairs, our pillows just happen to be the favorite colour of each of us. Sometimes the fact that we can "tell" George what we need just amazes us.*

We're overjoyed at seeing you, returned Morgan, *and we also have a favour to ask of you. We assume you've heard about Donald's alleged murder.*

Oh my yes! exclaimed Murphy. *Dreadful act. I simply don't know what makes some vile humans tick. And they call us animals!*

So true, sighed Morgan. *But your human George, as commissioner, may have information that might lead to capturing Donald's killer, even though he may not know it. George knows all about the bypass and the upcoming contract negotiations and Donald had confided that he had information for the commissioners that would affect those negotiations. It seems to be the only motive we can come up with. Do you think Donald had spoken with George?*

Well, said Mona, *Donald did stop by our house just last week. He and George had coffee in the kitchen, and they did talk about the bypass. But seriously, what they were speaking about meant little to us. They talked about easements, zoning, all-weather materials and hazardous conditions, and oh yes, he mentioned that several businesses, one in particular, objected to the traffic diversion.*

Hmmm, mused Morgan. *Did you happen to hear which business was the most vocal in its opposition?*

Well, answered Mac, *I didn't really listen to that part of the conversation. But I do remember hearing something about grain or hay.*

Mo shook her head. *I supposed they were trying not to commit libel or something. Humans can be hard to gauge as they dance about each other and spout legal mumbo jumbo that confounds even the smartest of them. Did George act surprised at anything Donald said, or did Donald ask George about upcoming talks with contractors, the county or the state?*

Well, Murphy confided, *George did say that he couldn't believe anyone would go out of their way to try to foil the bypass coming to fruition. George, as you know, has lobbied for the bypass for many years. He says it will benefit both the residents and the businesses in Seven Oaks, Dundee and Newberg. But perhaps there are people who, for whatever reason, don't want the residents and businesses here to prosper. Or maybe there are bidding wars for* the contracts? There could be so many things that you wouldn't ordinarily think of that could sink the project if someone really wanted it to.

We won't have time to hash all of this out today, quipped Mo, *because Kate will be coming back for us soon. Would you three put your heads together and formulate a few hypotheses from the conversation between George and Donald? We need to start somewhere, and since you could hear Donald's voice while they discussed this issue and you are so sensitive to variations in those sounds and his mannerisms, you're in the best positions to come up with a potential reason for all of this. I'll make sure Kate brings me back tomorrow. You know we're telepathic. Drives her nuts, but it serves both our purposes well.*

We'll do our best. Mac, Murphy and I are a good team. We'll put hour heads together; three heads are better than one any day!

Thank you, Mona, Mac and Murphy, said Georgia. *I don't think I will have time to properly vet Rebecca to make her aware to bring me to Cats Pause to see Mo tomorrow, as we don't share that same telepathic connection. And she is sooo busy with Junior and her new business.*

But I'll be thinking of ways to help you all! See you soon.

Just then, Kate pulled up in front of George's home. All the cats meandered down the sidewalk, and Mo and Georgia jumped into the back seat of the Mini. Much meowing was to be heard by the neighbors as the feline friends parted.

CINCO DE MEOW

Chapter 13 –

To some blind souls all cats are much alike. To a cat lover every cat from the beginning of time has been utterly and amazingly unique. *Jenny de Vries*

The buzz surrounding Oregon pinot noir and Oregon wines had been kicked up another notch. A major wine magazine gave 250 wines from Oregon a score of 90 or better. It was the kind of news that winemakers across the Willamette Valley were greeting with raised glasses.

Oregon wines had reached the tipping point in the national consciousness of wine drinkers, where consumers had become familiar enough with Oregon wines or Oregon as a prime wine-growing region that they were seeking out its wines.

Sommeliers tended to see it as a source of pinot noir in which the general style was more attuned to what they knew from Burgundy, than the wine they think of coming from California. There had been a gradual increase in interest and respect over the past decade.

In 2003, the same wine magazine had written of the increasing quality of American pinot noir, and told the parallel stories of the grape in California and Oregon. The two states got equal billing. However, a string of vintages from 2008-2010 had established a benchmark that may have been another tipping point. And it all happened during the great recession. Oregon wineries and tasting room sales were up twenty percent during the most difficult time in the economy. It was now accepted that the Willamette/Yamhill Valley was the leader over Burgundy and California.

One of the possible reasons for the growing popularity of Oregon pinot noir and increased attention given to the state's wines was the shift in taste of the wine consumer. People were shifting from the heavier reds to the brighter balanced and more nuanced flavors of Oregon pinot noir. Another reason for

CINCO DE MEOW

Oregon's pinot noir popularity was the quality of Oregon's wines. Oregon is blessed with a variety of geography that produces fantastic pinot noirs in the Willamette Valley, beautiful syrahs and other hearty reds in Southern Oregon, and remarkable merlots in Eastern Oregon.

In addition, there had been an active movement to provide education for vineyard managers and winemakers at Chemeketa and other community colleges, and at OSU and other major Oregon universities. The Chemeketa Northwest Viticulture Studies Center and other venues offered many wines in a reunion, meeting, wedding and party forum. Oregonians who had the right vineyard setting, education and the pioneering spirit had matched the quality of any region in the world.

Vineyard managers and winemakers in Oregon finally had enough collective experience, they'd learned how to make adjustments to overcome the challenges that Mother Nature throws at them in order to produce great quality wine. "We learn from each other, and we share notes. And we've had enough opportunities to learn. High scores help build our reputation, but our goal is to produce quality wines and not just scores," countered John Ferguson.

"As part of the entire U.S. wine industry, Oregon production of wines is still a drop in the bucket. We're not making enough wine, but this is not a problem – as long as you don't disappoint an established customer.

The good news is that there's still enough vineyard land available to cultivate and we are just at the beginning point of a great industry for Oregon.

If you can just imagine what the Willamette Valley wine industry will be like 50 or 100 years from now, it will be breathtaking. The growth is in front of us.

CINCO DE MEOW

Kats Jory Hills Vineyard

"Oregonians seem to be the best ambassadors for our wine industry. Oregon consumers are proud of Oregon wines. People buy Oregon wines to give as gifts to people in other states. They want to tell the Oregon success story. They are the most convincing method of getting the word out about Oregon wines. We have a very strong chorus of supporters that's helping attract attention. And hopefully, that chorus will grow."

Kate Ferguson had mixed emotions today. She was feeling buoyant about the quality of Kats Jory Hills Estate wines and their promise for the upcoming Cinco de Mayo celebration, but the death of Donald Jenkins left her feeling heavy and unsettled, more unbalanced than she had ever felt.

She and Mary Malone were spending the day on final preparations for the event, but Kate couldn't shake the feeling that she could be doing more to help find Donald's killer; she needed to feel that she was doing all she could do, or why else exist, if only to do for oneself?

To make matters worse, Mo had been jittery all morning, pawing, scratching no apparent itches, squealing like a pig, and generally misbehaving to the point that Kate was ready to take her to the shelter just to silence whatever protests were going on in her feline mind.

But Kate really missed Morgan when they weren't together, so she kept a stiff upper lip and worked even harder with Mary for the good of the winery.

"Mary," said Kate, still biting her lip, "I just feel so useless. I know there is more to be done to help Charles and Company find

Donald's killer, but I can't make myself move any faster. The cats seem to be anxious to get together and I have a feeling they know something, or at least they have the resolve and the audacity to try and discover the reasons for this hideous crime."

"Now, Kate," replied Mary. "You know those cats just enjoy being around each other, and I just can't quite believe they are enjoying themselves in the quest to solve Donald's stabbing death."

"Why not?" queried Kate, rearranging for the fifth time the colorful centerpiece on the tasting bar. "Animals have a keen sense of danger; they are survivors, born to vet signs of danger for real threats. I have a feeling the cats sensed something at the Knightly Ranch that even Charles and his detectives could never fathom. Have you seen the way they caterwaul when they see each other? I think there's more to that music than singing!"

Mary didn't have a response for that because she had long wondered if Kate truly understood those cats, but still, she didn't want to upset her friend any further by openly doubting her communication skills – or her sanity. "Kate, you could be on to something.

Nonetheless, let's wrap up our decorating and prepping, and maybe make a stop at the McMinnville Police Station to see if Charles can have lunch. Between the two of us, we're likely to shake something loose that we haven't seen before."

"Good idea, Mary," replied Kate. "I've almost completed the checklist. I need to call the caterers and ready the lighting. I do love these new electric candles. So much safer than wax, they burn longer, and they give off the same warm glow as wax candles without smoke or heat. I have all the tables readied with checkered cloth and I've made certain that olive oil and wine vinegar are on each table for the wonderful ciabatta we'll be serving."

Kate had decided that thirty bar-height tables should be sufficient to keep the traffic moving along the tasting and pouring bar. Although only two chairs surrounded each table, the space was comfortable enough to stand next to the chairs and lean on the tables, with plenty of room on each for small plates of food, bread for dipping, and of course, several glasses of wine.

"I'd better give Charles a call first, just in case he's out on assignment," mused Kate.

"Charles hates surprises, but I do think he'd want to be available for lunch if at all possible. Should we invite James?"

"I think that would be spot on," cried Mary. "James and I have been enjoying each other's company three or four nights a week, and if he doesn't have a crushing schedule today at the clinic, I know he'd love to see you and Charles. I'll give him a call to see how his morning is going. I am supposed to work at the clinic this afternoon for three or four hours, so if he's not finished with paperwork, I can certainly make that up for him."

"Brilliant," countered Kate. "We're ready for Cinco de Mayo, and we can also discuss the arrangements for tomorrow evening's event. Charles mentioned that he and James would be renting a town car and driver, not just for us, but in case there are any slightly inebriated patrons, we'll have the limousine and a sober driver to take them home."

"Well," Mary smirked, "I would doubt too many people will drink heavily when they're being served and monitored by the best law enforcement officers this area has to offer!"

CINCO DE MEOW

Chapter 14 –

An ordinary kitten will ask more questions than any five year old. *Carl Van Vechten*

Charles offered to meet his three friends at their favorite bistro for lunch. He'd had a few things to complete, the most important was the interviewing of everyone who had visited the Knightly Ranch within the several days prior to the murder.

He had spoken with Andrew Knightly, of course, and also with Kate, the Medical Examiner, and other police officers who had responded to the scene. There were at least three farm workers who were somewhere on the ranch that morning, and Charles sought them out for questioning. He couldn't believe that no one saw or heard anything, or that no one was aware whether Donald had enemies.

"Jaime," Charles spoke as he motioned Jaime to a chair, "I need to ask you a few questions about Donald Jenkins. If you wish to have an official translator here, I can arrange that in short measure." Charles and Jaime, one of Andrew Knightly's three ranch workers, sat in a comfortable office in the Knightly barn. All three of Andrew's ranch workers had migrated from Mexico to California and then to Oregon, and all three had chosen to settle at the ranch for year-around work. As with many older migrant farmworkers, the three men had little time to go to school to learn English, but they wanted to learn and did learn a fair amount from the ranch owner, the community and from Olivia. Translation, though, can be tricky if not done properly, as many Spanish words had similar sounds and meanings and could be misinterpreted.

"No, señor," replied Jamie quietly, "that will not be necessary. I have learned much English and am proud to say that I have recently acquired my citizenship. I am happy to speak with you in my second language. I will do all in my power to help you find Donald's killer. He was an excellent man."

Charles liked Jaime and his two co-workers, Juan and Paco. They treated the horses as though they belonged to each of them, and they truly loved their jobs at the ranch and the ranch owner as well. Jaime was sort of the lead worker for the migrants, as he had been with Andrew the longest and knew the most about the ranch. He had painstakingly made time to attend citizenship classes in McMinnville three nights each week. Although many of the classes were delivered in Spanish, the text books were printed in English, and Jaime was proud that he was able to read now in that language. He had graduated from la escuela secondaria in Nuevo Leon, Mexico, had a quick mind and was anxious to learn American ways and language.

"Did you notice anything unusual early on the morning Donald was killed, Jamie?" asked Charles. "Any new faces or sounds that might have registered as unusual at the time, or any activity that was out of the ordinary?"

"No, Lieutenant Beltz, I was up at four o'clock in the morning, went about feeding the horses and letting some of them out to the pasture. I saw Donald arrive early, too, but I didn't see him after about 4:30. The horses were somewhat, what is the word, *agitated*, but that sometimes happens when the owls are mating or when delivery trucks come into the ranch. We had hay and grain delivery that morning before the sun rose in the sky."

"The horses were agitated? Is a delivery that early unusual?" asked Charles. "And please, Jaime, call me 'Charles'."

"No, Charles," answered Jaime with a smile, "early farm deliveries happen all the time. It helps to have the delivery trucks in and out, deliveries put away before the horses are out in the paddocks and before equipment starts moving around the ranch."

"Did you see the delivery truck driver?" queried Charles. "Was he the usual driver or do different drivers bring in food for the horses?"

"Well," replied Jaime, "we have a new hay and grain distributor, as our previous distributor, West Coast, sold the company. That would have been only our second delivery by Western Hay and Grain Company, and I did not see the driver."

"Well, thanks, Jaime," said Charles. "Please let me know if you think of anything that might help us find Donald's killer. I'm sure you don't feel safe, either, with this villain walking the fields."

"No señor," said Jaime. "I will do all I can to assist you, and I will contact you if I remember anything else that might help you."

"You've been a great help already, Jaime," said Charles. "Thank you for your time. Here's my card, and please call me any time."

Jaime left, and Charles interviewed Juan and Paco separately. Both men were nervous being questioned, as they knew little English and they'd had their share of bad experiences with corrupt law enforcement in Nuevo Leon. Both had families in Mexico, and both worked hard to earn enough to perhaps bring those families to Oregon in the future.

Charles learned nothing new from the ranch hands, except that each confirmed that there had been an early grain delivery the day Donald was killed, and no one had seen the driver. Paco had struggled the most with the interview, and did not make eye contact with Charles. Charles knew this was common for migrant farmworkers when confronted with law enforcement in this country. Juan and Paco had tried to keep a very low profile and do their best work just to avoid this kind of attention. Still, Charles had tried to gain their trust, and although Juan seemed to relax and concentrate on answering the questions, Paco remained distant.

Charles drove slowly to the restaurant. He had a chilling feeling about Donald's death and the manner in which he had been killed. It didn't seem logical that Donald's killer could just slip in and sneak out of the ranch without anyone seeing or hearing anything.

CINCO DE MEOW

Chapter 15 –

This is a cat's world; we just live in it. *Brooke Leigh Williams*

As every cat owner knows, nobody owns a cat. *Ellen Perry Berkeley*

    Kate, James and Mary arrived at the restaurant before the appointed time, and they had much to talk about as they waited for Charles. They had scored a cozy little table near the window, and at this hour, the restaurant was buzzing with diners.

    "James," said Mary, "Kate and I have been postulating about a motive for Donald's alleged murder. We've talked about the usual suspects, family or friends, and we just don't find anyone who disliked Donald. We don't think he had any enemies. What little family he had is living somewhere on the East Coast, and around here, everyone liked Donald. I'm anxious to hear Charles' take on this, too. Donald was just a likeable guy who had a way with animals and who worked very hard, at least the entire time he's been here in the Yamhill Valley."

"Mary and Kate," replied James, "I have no doubt you've left no stone unturned already in your quest to find Donald's killer. But let's not get in Charles' way. This is serious business. I, too, am waiting to hear if Charles has turned anything up yet. Anything he can tell us about, that is."

"I think we all can agree that Charles is on top of this investigation," said Kate. "He's barely getting any sleep and he told me that even when he nods off, he'll awaken with thoughts of some clue he may have missed or some motive he's overlooked. Very frustrating for him, and I totally understand the need to avoid meddling."

"Well," said James, "I wouldn't call it 'meddling,' but Charles is very meticulous in lining up evidence and doing his research and combing through clues and lab results. He'll no doubt solve this in due time, but this little town will not feel secure until he does."

James and Mary nodded to each other and moved just a bit closer together. The restaurant was so cozy, and being among friends always gave Mary a warm glow. She looked at Kate, recognizing that Kate was expectantly sitting on the edge of her chair waiting for Charles. How lucky we are, Mary thought, to have found two such wonderful men to keep us company. From her experience, truly nice guys were few and far between. In their age group, most men were married, and those who weren't had sometimes been through several divorces, and had become serial daters – with the assistance of online dating sites. Yes, Mary reflected, we are truly blessed with James and Charles.

"I see Charles down the street," said Kate. "It'll likely take him a bit to arrive here, as he knows everyone, and people stop to speak to him all the time. Very unusual, I think, because the uniform on other local law enforcers can serve to intimidate people. Not so with Charles, I guess. I think that comes from his years as a community liaison, before he became a lieutenant. Look, he's got four people chatting him up and he's so polite."

Charles was enjoying himself, and he was never the type to demand respect. He believed in earning it. Over the years, he had proven himself to be straight forward and very adept at his job, so the townspeople flocked to him and enjoyed his company. They knew he was looking out for their best interests, and he had never disappointed them. Charles never liked to rush people, except at times when he was interrogating, of course, so he enjoyed his time and that served to make people enjoy their time spent with him, too.

Charles eventually disengaged himself from the group, and made his way to the restaurant. As he reached the front door, he heard George King calling his name. George hurried his step and reached Charles before he entered the restaurant.

"Charles," panted George, "I'm not as young as I used to be. Let me catch my breath. Whew! Are you meeting friends here for lunch?"

"I am, George," replied Charles. "You are welcome to join us, too."

"Well, I appreciate that, Charles, but my wife is waiting lunch for me at home," said George. "I just wanted to tell run a few things by you regarding Donald's death and the bypass situation."

"If you don't have time this instant, George, why don't you come by my office in about an hour?" asked Charles. "That'll give me time to fuel up and get back to McMinnville. I could use some fresh interchange while I'm awaiting all the lab results in this case."

"Will do, Charles. I'll fuel up, too, and I'll see you maybe a little past two o'clock." George ambled down the street to his car and waved back at Charles as he started his engine. He was never late to lunch as his round belly might attest, especially when his wife was cooking one of her delicious meals, and he loved seeing the cats in the middle of the day, too.

Charles finally opened the door to the Red Barn Bistro to join his friends.

After greetings were shared all around, Charles sat down finally in the chair Kate had reserved for him. It took them a few minutes to chat about the weather and to peruse the menu, but then they began their discussion of the topic on all their minds, Donald's 'murder.'

CINCO DE MEOW

"I haven't been able to sleep a wink," admitted Kate as she finished deciding on her lunch choice. "I can't for the life of me figure out why anyone would want to kill poor Donald."

"I've just spoken with the ranch hands at Knightly Ranch," said Charles. "I didn't find anything that popped out at me, but Jaime and the other ranch hands told me that there was a grain delivery that morning. However, Jaime followed by stating that there was nothing unusual about an early morning delivery, as they preferred getting the hay and grain out of the yard and into the bins and storage before too much traffic muddied the open ground and damaged the food. The only thing new or different about the delivery was that Andrew is using a new distributor, after his previous grain company sold out. But they are basically the same operation, perhaps with new or combined personnel. I'll be checking that out this afternoon."

"You know," volunteered James, "Donald told Kate he had information that might affect the 99W Diversion project. Could that be significant?"

"Perhaps," replied Charles. "Kate did mention that Donald told her he felt the information might upset certain people in the area, but he didn't elaborate as to how or why that would happen. I'm going to speak with George King this afternoon, and maybe he'll have some more to add to Donald's supposed exposé."

"Well, I can't imagine what it could be," said Mary. "Almost every business and residence in the area approves of the interchange. The diversion will be good for local businesses."

"So we all think," said Charles. "It may be that one of those business owners disagrees, although except for assigning the contracting, the time has come and passed to vocalize that disagreement as the project is approved and off the drawing board. It could also be that whatever Donald knew was more than passing along a disagreement. He may have stumbled on something that we don't know about because it was important enough to keep under wraps."

"I can't imagine what that would be about," said Kate. "The interchange proposal has been around for years and years. Why would someone or some business just now oppose it?"

"I can't tell you that because I don't know," said Charles with a smile. "Kate, let's enjoy our lunch and talk of other issues. We certainly have much to talk about what with Cinco de Mayo event coming up. Besides, I'm famished. Here's our server. Kate, be my guest."

Kate ordered, then Mary, followed by the two men. They began discussing the upcoming event that certainly was also on their minds. Time had flown, and the event was just days away. Kate and Mary felt prepared, but Kate's father, John, had come down with a serious cold and Kate was concerned it might turn into pneumonia. She had been visiting him every few hours, taking him soup and making certain he drank lots of water. She thought his fever had broken, but John still resisted going to the doctor. Kate told the group that if John was still feeling punk this afternoon, he could just forget further resistance. She had made an appointment with John's doctor, and had told the nurse about John's apparent lack of concern for his health. Of course, she made the call out of John's earshot, so he wasn't aware of the pending appointment until the time came to put him in the car.

"You know your father can be a challenge when it comes to keeping commitments other than in the wine business," quipped Mary to Kate's attention. "He is stubborn, much like someone else at this table when it comes to mundane doctor visits."

"I beg your pardon, Mary," countered Kate, "but that was only one time and I was in the middle of building the B&B, with vendors waiting on me for direction. What a bother taking blood tests and being poked and prodded. It was just a cold and I knew it would wear itself out."

"That cold lasted a month," replied Mary, "and you were exhausted day after day. It cleared very soon after Dr. Jones prescribed the Z-Pak, and even at that, we had to pester you to take the darned pills."

"In any case," said Kate changing the subject to a topic away from her temperament, "dad will be seeing the doctor today if he's still got the cough. Although he can't be serving folks all sick and puny, he won't want to miss this event. He loves to socialize, and he's so proud of this year's vintage and his barrels are brimming with delicious new wine. I think he'll see reason. Oh, here are our lunches. Last one done is a fool!"

"Although I hate to complain, I'm so hungry I can't focus on more than one thing at a time, so let's eat and continue our day," said Charles. "I'll stop by this afternoon late and see if I can help you ladies wrap up the preparations. John should be in bed resting, but I can do a lot of the lifting and hauling in his stead."

Chapter 16 –

A cat pours his body on the floor like water. It is restful just to see him. *William Lyon Phelps*

It takes a long time to make a great winegrowing region. The Jory Hills creation started about 15 to 17 million years ago when in far eastern Washington very fluid lava erupted and flowed west over the northern part of what is now the Willamette Valley. During this period, basaltic lava flowed right over the top of the Jory Hills, because at that point, the hills did not exist.

Starting about five million years ago, mass tectonic uplift started to occur, as the North American plate slipped under the Pacific plate. This created what is now the Coast Range of

Oregon, southwest Washington and northern California.

One of the many ripple effects of all of this land movement was the uplift of a single landmass which rose up from above the now northern Willamette Valley floor, creating this very special place these vineyards and wineries call home...the Jory (or 'Red' as they are also called) Hills.

Further defining this appellation were the catastrophic Missoula Floods. These floods happened between 15,500 and 12,700 years ago, on the interval of one flood every 60 to 90 years. The floods were caused by a glacier heading south clogging rivers near Missoula, Montana. Lake Missoula would grow into a very large lake, and every 60 to 90 years would break through the ice dam rushing down from Montana into and eventually filling the Willamette Valley to a depth of 300 to 330 feet. As each of these floods receded, a small layer of sediment was laid down over the Willamette Valley, covering all elevations below 300 to 330 feet. This is where the definition of the Jory Hills became apparent. Anything below 300 to 330 feet was a sedimentary based soil, while anything remaining above that elevation remained predominantly Jory soil.

Kats Jory Hills Estate wines were among the finest in this valley, sharing the wonderful soil and climate perfect for growing pinot noir grapes. The Cinco de Mayo event would offer barrel tasting of new vintages, and of course, several varieties and bottling years of fine wines.

The time was now very close to this celebration, and with the help of many friends and family, the winery was ready for the event. With only hours to go, Kate and Mary had finished every detail, and were looking forward to the evening's festivities.

Casting a pall over their excitement for the event, of course, was Donald's death and the ongoing investigation. It didn't seem that they were any closer to solving the mystery of his death than they had been days ago.

But the friends and the cats vowed to go through the evening with smiles and merriment because the proceeds of the holiday event were pledged to such a wonderful cause – the shelter cats! – and they also vowed to continue their quest to help find Donald's killer as soon as they said the last goodbyes to their guests.

CINCO DE MEOW

Chapter 17–

Cats can work out mathematically the exact place to sit that will cause the most inconvenience. *Pam Brown*

When several of the cat friends were lucky enough to be adopted from Cats Pause Feline Shelter, their respective humans had promised to bring these felines together to see one another from time to time. As their parents were busy helping out with the event, the Kensington girls, Beatrice and Pippa, had dropped off Diana and Edward at Elizabeth Conley's home to visit with Phillip. Diana and Edward had been making such a racket caterwauling in the house that it was clear they needed a change of venue to lift their spirits. The three cats had met at Cats Pause while awaiting a furr-ever home, and they had become friends as only cats can be friends. They were also fortunate enough to be adopted by understanding humans, and they continued their friendship with many visits.

Diana, Edward! exclaimed Phillip. *It's been weeks since I've seen you, and I'm so grateful for the company. My mum, Elizabeth, has been so involved with printing fliers and posters for the Cinco de Mayo event, she has positively neglected me! You don't know how lonely it can be because you have each other!*

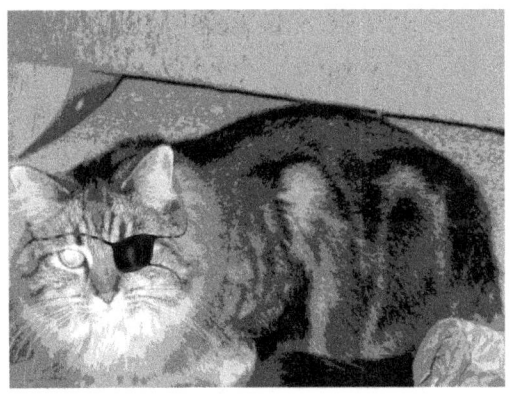

Phillip

Oh pshaw, hissed Diana, *look at this brand new climbing tree you have. And Elizabeth has installed shelves and bedding at all the windows. You have an endless movie going outside those windows!*

113

Still, pouted Philip, *I do miss you two – and all my other shelter friends, as well.*

Phillip had only one eye as a result of an encounter with a stick-bearing child, so it was sometimes necessary to swivel his head back and forth to see what the other cats could make out distinctly with a steady head and two eyes. The lack of an eye, though, never slowed Phillip down, and he never sat still for long. If he'd been allowed to go out of doors, those birds he watched all day long would disappear. Ultimately, a good enough reason to keep cats indoors, their cautious humans thought. Let them watch their birds through glass, and let the birds live to see another day and continue to provide entertainment.

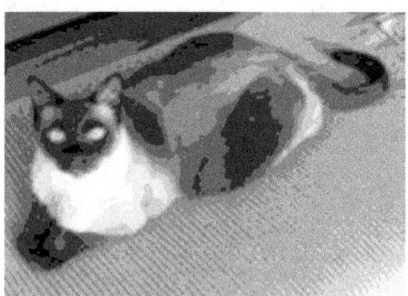

Diana

CINCO DE MEOW

Diana, a lovely Siamese girl, never understood Phillip's desire to move about all the time, and to constantly be surrounded by company. Certainly, Diana loved Edward and appreciated his company most of the time, but she appreciated also her privacy and more than once had clipped Edward's nose with her paw to let him know about it. Edward, for his attentiveness, was content to stay close to Diana's side – until she swiped at him. Then he would wander around rather aimlessly, wishing for the chance to go see Phillip, who shared the same lack of craving for privacy.

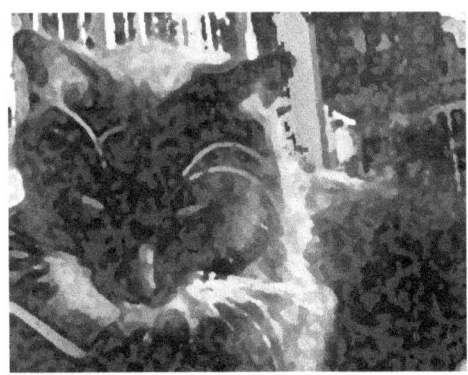

Edward

From what I understand, said Edward, *Mo has invited all of us to the Cinco de Mayo* event this evening. And we're even allowed to stay in the winery and view the festivities! Upon our last visit, Georgia told me that we will even be provided special tuna flakes so we can celebrate, too! It will be a wonderful Cinco de Meowwww!

Yes, replied Phillip, Elizabeth will take us to the ball, as it were, and because we'll be allowed inside the whole time, we can sleuth among the guests to sniff out what we can about Donald's death.

Tragic, that! cried Edward. Arbor and Syrah will be at the party, too. Between all of us, we should be able to give this investigation a good boost. The humans never try to hide anything when speaking around us because they can't fathom that we might understand what's going on in the world. How wrong they are! And how clueless they can be when it comes to our clue gathering. Why, we cats are meant for the hunt – and most especially when the hunt culminates with capture of a mouse or other prey – in this case, a criminal.

Sadly, said Diana, Lady and Señor will not be with us tonight, as Andrew Knightly is very concerned about their safety. Although he can't imagine who could have killed Donald, the fact that the crime occurred on his ranch has him all jittery. And poor Victoria hasn't been out of the house for her walk in a week. Lady says Victoria is getting lonely, but because she has no claws, she is destined to stay indoors for her own safety. I wonder if Elizabeth would consider bringing Victoria home to keep Phillip company? You know, Victoria hasn't had the chance to blossom since Lady and Señor found her in the back of a delivery truck.

Oh! exclaimed Phillip. *I would so love that! She must be lonely, too. She could always visit with Miss Lades and Señor when we all see each other. Oh, let's plant that idea. Elizabeth is somewhat receptive to my "suggestions," so maybe I can impress upon her how much I'd love Victoria's company. Besides, with feline company, she wouldn't have to worry so much that I'll escape the front door and capture the birds.*

Agreed, said Diana and Edward simultaneously. *Let's all think our hardest as soon as Elizabeth gets us in the car. Somehow that seems to be a good place for humans to reflect. And three cats focusing on her mind at the same time should be able to plant a very large seed.*

So the Three Mouseketeers spent the rest of the afternoon planning their strategy. Hopefully, Victoria would be as excited as Phillip about the move!

CINCO DE MEOW

Chapter 18 –

Everything I know I learned from my cat. When you're
hungry, eat. When you're tired, nap in a sunbeam. When
you go to the vet's, pee on your owner. *Gary Smith*

   George King sat at his computer desk,
staring out the window in disbelief. How could I
have missed this for so long? George had
received a phone call late that morning from a
proactive citizen who had expressed concern
that certain events may be transpiring because
Western Grain's property sat directly on the
proposed route of the Highway 99 bypass.
Apparently, a friend of a friend of a friend had
reported to the caller that grain trucks were
moving in and out of the property at all hours,
especially in the dead of night. Of course, if the

grain was being moved long distances, an early start with little traffic would be prudent. He pondered the conversation and shook his head at the revelation that should have come weeks ago.

And then there was the midnight revelation that simply "came to him out of the blue." Of course, unbeknownst to George, that revelation was likely because Mona, Mac and Murphy were simultaneously 'thinking' of the subject, and had coaxed George to think and think about possible motives for Donald's killing. After all, Donald had mentioned his concern about grain issues during his last visit with George; unfortunately, George had dismissed those concerns as impossible to happen or to prove.

Hazzah! mused George as more 'out-of-the-blue' thoughts crowded his mind. No one seems to have seriously considered the GMO factor!

Genetically modified organisms hadn't been on his list of motives for much of anything happening in the valley. The government had a cadre of people who were responsible for monitoring and testing for GMOs in the agricultural community. The most recent testing had been done several months ago, and no evidence of modified grain was discovered. How then, could a company like Western Grain potentially cover up a whole warehouse full of the high-yield modified grain?

Western Grain now delivered feed and grain to most of the local ranchers and farmers. No one really knew the new owners, but they didn't live in Oregon. Currently, their office told callers that at least one of the owners would be present at the Seven Oaks facility roughly one week each month, and they scheduled those visits only to wrap up any unfinished business or to sign any required papers for the government. Appointments could be made, but they were few and far between during that one week when the owners needed to complete business.

At this juncture, no one really knew or understood the effects of GMOs on livestock. More to the point, most ranchers insisted that there be transparency in marketing and selling grains and hay. Even if there were no immediate repercussions visible in the use of genetically modified grains, the research wasn't complete as to the long-term effects. Why, then, couldn't the grain distributors wait for such research to be completed and findings published?

The answer to that question was quite simple. GMOs were easier to grow because they were hardier, and harvests were much more abundant. Their seed structures had been modified to resist pestilence, drought and excessive rainfall, pitfalls to farmers in the Pacific Northwest. The harvests were more lucrative, plants growing faster and larger so that more product was available quicker. But at what cost to livestock and humans? That was the question that hadn't yet been answered to the satisfaction of the ranchers. So until it was, farmers were choosing to stick with what they knew and the statistics that were available. Of course, there were always a few who might be driven by greed to sell GMO-based products to consumers without benefit of disclosure. The farmers had to trust that their feed distributors were honest, and most had proven themselves to be so with years of serving the local farm community with the finest grains grown the old fashioned way.

The GMO controversy came to light most glaringly when it was discovered a few years prior that a ranch in Eastern Oregon was growing GMO wheat, although it claimed that perhaps the GMOs were introduced accidentally by wind-carried seed. At the crux of that discovery was the cancelation by the Japanese of import contracts relating to Oregon wheat products. The Japanese weren't willing to trust that only that particular farm was growing and selling GMO enhanced feed. Such a furor ensued that Oregon farmers had taken great pains to prove they planted traditional grains for harvest.

Western Grain, under the previous company name, West Coast Feed and Seed, had long stood at the crossroads of the Highway 99 Bypass. But when its owners decided to call it quits and sell the company and distributorship, some of the integrity counted on by the farmers in Yamhill Valley was diminished, if only because face-to-face meetings with the "outsiders" was difficult to arrange. The new owners put on a virtuous front, and it was hard to accuse them of any wrongdoing because the deliveries were timely, the grain appeared to be a quality product and looked entirely the same as grain delivered by the former owners.

So Western Grain stockpiled grain purchased mainly from Idaho and Northern

California, where GMO testing and monitoring was not considered a priority. Those two states especially were more concerned with water shortages than the possibility that some farmers were growing GMO wheat and hay.

George King knew all of this was rumored after the Japanese grain debacle, but he had no proof that Western Grain was selling GMO products to local farmers. Perhaps Donald had only scratched the surface with his discovery of what he thought was pertinent information related to a possible cover-up at Western Grain. Was that discovery enough to warrant a murder? George didn't know for sure, but it was the only motive he could conjure up to explain the tragic death.

George knew that one or more of the new Western Grain administration would be present at the Cinco de Mayo celebration that evening. Maybe this would be a good time to confront them with the conundrum. Is Western Hay and Grain selling local ranchers GMO product? Would zoning for the company change due to the completion of the Highway 99 Bypass? Would government inspectors show up soon to establish a standard at the local level? George vowed to ask these questions that night, and he would discuss his views with Charles. After he finished mulling the situation over, he set about the daily task (which he enjoyed) of preparing early dinner for the trio of felines he so loved. They would accompany him to the event, and he hoped they would enjoy their visits with their feline friends. They were an odd bunch, and could always be counted upon to cheer him up when stress and anxiety started to take over.

When George had spoken with Charles several days prior, he had passed on Donald's concerns regarding Western Grain. Charles had advised him that Donald had given Kate similar information. But although he had mentioned Donald's accusation regarding possible GMO contamination, he minimized it verbally as "only a guess on Donald's part." Well, this has to be the motive for Donald's demise: there wasn't anything else that could possibly have been so important, and Donald had told him that it was a secret and that someone might be mightily upset if it was brought to light. Well, thought George (although he was also talking out loud to himself), I'll have to call Charles and recant my misgivings on the GMO subject especially.

It's important to at least investigate this as possible motive for Donald's death!

CINCO DE MEOW

Chapter 19 –

I've noticed that what cats most appreciate in a human being is not the ability to produce food which they take for granted – but his or her entertainment value. *Geoffrey Household*

Mona, Mac and Murphy had listened very carefully as George mumbled to himself. They didn't think George realized he was speaking quite animatedly out loud, but they sat quietly looking out the window so they wouldn't disturb George's thoughts. They agreed that George had offered the most likely scenario.

CINCO DE MEOW

Soon, Charles, responding to George's frantic call, knocked at his back door, and the two began discussing George's suspicions over coffee. The cats could be seen peering at the two humans from perches all over the room. At one point, Charles smoothed his hair down as a vague "suggestion" that Donald's killer might attend the gala occurred to him. The three pair of eyes trained on him made him feel quite watched, and although his back was to them, he could feel those eyes and new questions gnawed at him.

Charles spoke to George as he turned and looked around the room, spying the cats spying on him.

CINCO DE MEOW

"George," spoke Charles, "I think you may have hit upon the crux of this investigation. The motive for Donald's killing may well have been his knowledge of something like we've been discussing, a GMO buy-and-sell cover-up, and the need to silence Donald to allow their operation to continue unnoticed."

"Well, I can't take credit for the entire idea. Initially, I had dismissed Donald's concerns. But I swear these darned cats plant ideas in my head while I'm sleeping. Or when I'm sitting quietly reading the newspaper. Or just about any other time they feel the need to bother me. Sometimes one of them will sit on the couch next to me, or (don't tell anyone about this) sit on the kitchen table and just stare at me for what seems like hours. When I look at them, it appears they are looking at a bug on the wall just behind my head, but when I resume whatever I was doing, I'll catch them looking directly at my eyes. Makes my hair stand on end sometimes."

Charles now knew that feeling as he had just experienced it. "Well, I think we're allowing our imaginations to run away with us. In any case, although I respect your role as commissioner in this matter, I'd like to talk to a representative from Western Grain myself. If I'm right, I'll get that chance tonight. I don't want to tip my hand, so I'll employ very light interrogation techniques that are more in keeping with party conversation than true interrogation."

"OK, Charles," replied George. "I won't interfere with your investigation, as I have utmost confidence that you will get to the bottom of this. After you've 'spoken' with them, though, I still want to interview one or more of the owners about the GMO issue for the newspaper. I just can't for the life of me consider that even a covert operation of the nature we've been speaking, would be sufficient cause for murder."

"You never know when the almighty dollar takes precedence over the Almighty," said Charles. "One man's sin is another man's heroic deed. And it may be we're completely on the wrong track. Let's just see what tonight brings – if one or more of Western Grain's owners and operators attend the event."

Charles thanked George for the coffee and for sharing his ideas. He arose from his chair and placed his cup in George's sink. When he turned toward the door, he noticed that cats were busy licking their paws and preening, looking as if they hadn't a care in the world.

The cats, for their part, were digesting the overheard conversation and looking as bored as possible. They would take this information with them to the winery event this evening where they would share with their sleuthing comrades. They vowed silently to get to the bottom of this case and to avenge Donald's death by exposing his killer.

CINCO DE MEOW

Chapter 20 –

There are many intelligent species in the universe. They are all owned by cats. *Anonymous*

Arbor and Syrah rode in high style to the winery in the dazzling Spay Station. Mo warmly greeted Georgia who arrived with Rebecca. Lawrence Jr. was not in attendance, having scored both Beatrice and Pippa Kensington as babysitters for the evening. Mona, Mac and Murphy arrived with the Kings, and literally shot out of their carriers and into the winery to seek their friends.

Diana, Edward and Phillip applied their super-strength efforts at telepathy relentlessly in the backseat of Elizabeth's car for the entire drive to the event. Elizabeth found herself thinking about poor Victoria being all alone at the ranch during the day when the other cats and humans were outside or at their respective jobs. How odd that I'm thinking of Victoria, she mused. But she must remember to ask Olivia and Andrew about the possibility of allowing Victoria to stay with her, at least during the daytime. It would be a good thing for all of them, but especially for poor Phillip who was not above howling with displeasure when he didn't get enough attention from her. (While Elizabeth pondered her desire to help little Victoria, Phillip, Diana and Edward literally jumped for joy at their success in winning mind games from the back seat.) Little Victoria would be a welcome addition, Elizabeth thought, and would most likely help quiet her home down to normal decibels. By the time they all arrived at the winery, Elizabeth was quite convinced she needed to expand her feline household.

Three very smug and satisfied cats stepped lightly into the winery, tails high, and headed for the gaggle of friends circulating around the "cat side" of the room. They couldn't wait to share their triumph with the friends waiting there and looked forward to hearing more information from their buddies.

Also, there were lovely dishes of feline morsels, and several intricate cat trees (literally), one that reached ten feet in height. What a fabulous cat adventure this would be!

The cats noted that food was provided for the humans, too.

At least fifty people had arrived by this time, and were chatting noisily. William Kent and John Ferguson had entered the forum about the same time as the Kensingtons, and it seemed the entire McMinnville Police Department was on hand. John had visited the doctor's office at Kate's insistence, and was rewarded with feeling much better after hearing he did not have pneumonia, nor the flu. The doctor did prescribe antibiotics, which he had taken immediately, and some decongestants to clear his head. He actually felt human again, but he would be careful to work the room all the while keeping his distance from guests' drinks and food.

The limo sat primly outside the side doors, and the driver hired for the night was already enjoying catered delicacies – and iced tea.

Anticipation was in the air, and what with wine being served at the bar and at the tables, and the lovely trays of scrumptious food that sat in strategic spots literally everywhere in the room, the evening promised fun and adventure for cat and human alike.

CINCO DE MEOW

Chapter 21 –

With their qualities of cleanliness, discretion, affection, patience, dignity, and courage, how many of us I ask you, would be capable of becoming cats? *Fernand Mery*; <u>Her Majesty the Cat</u>

As the event reached full swing, the feline and human friends began separately lamenting the loss of Donald. Someone in the human group proposed a toast, and everyone held a moment of silence in Donald's memory. A box at the front of the room was filled with donations for Donald's memorial service, as he apparently had no family locally and never spoke specifically of anyone anywhere else though he had said he hailed from 'back east.'

CINCO DE MEOW

Kats Jory Hills Estate Tasting Room

Thus, the evening was perfect in all respects but the one, the loss of one of their own. The trio that played soft violin and guitar music entertained the group while Mary and Kate helped James and Charles bring more food from the industrial coolers. John Ferguson had never seen the winery so packed with people, and he was very pleased that so many turned out for the event, considering the pall of Donald's recent death hanging in their midst. Because John's cold had taken the amazing sabbatical, he could finally enjoy himself and his success. His strength was back, and the energy he emanated as he circulated through the room was that of a twenty-year-old.

William Kent took groups on winery tours, and relished the chance to explain all about winemaking and the wine district in general. Some of the charm of the Yamhill Valley, as an extension of the Willamette Valley, was its geologic history, and William was well-versed in that history. His rendition of how the silt and soil was created by volcanic conditions in the Dundee Hills appellation, and thus in Seven Oaks, kept his tour groups mesmerized.

William noted as he led one group to what they called 'the caves,' "The Dundee Hills appellation is an area famous for red clay-loam soils that were deposited here by ancient lava flows. The Dundee Hills American Viticultural Area is Oregon's first micro-AVA, and is over 80% "Jory" soil-type. This special volcanic soil has excellent minerality and drainage. Also, the Dundee Hills benefit from being drier and warmer than many pockets that surround it. All of these factors together combine to showcase unique characteristics found in the best pinot noirs from this region. The wines tend to be very focused with great clarity and complexity. Some of the descriptors are bright red fruits, exotic spices, and a gorgeous minerality in the structure.

"The volcanic Jory soils of the Dundee Hills are ideally suited to production of world-class wines. The pinot noirs are rich and complex with supple tannins while the chardonnays are vibrant, mineral-scented and possess great structure.

"The Jory soils, covering the mid and upper elevations of the valley were formed from ancient volcanic basalt. These volcanic deposits originated from lava flows over 15 million years ago, before the hills were actually formed by plate movement in the Pacific.

"Jory soils are typically 4-6 feet in depth and consist of a brick colored silty, clay loam. The depth and qualify of the soils lend themselves ideally to the practice of viticulture. Grapevines' roots are encouraged to grow deep into the earth, while the rich soils nourish the vines. These exceptional growing conditions produce consistently excellent wines."

William had a million stories, and his knowledge of the geological and geographical wonders of the Willamette Valley was vast. Several of the guests joined more than one tour, as many had more questions they hadn't the chance to ask the first time around.

As the evening glided on, the guests shared their experiences in wine country, but also continued discussing with each other various knowledge and best guesses about the circumstances of Donald's death. Of course, the amateur human sleuths in the room boasted their solutions to the crime.

The cats circulated quietly amongst the guests, absorbing hints and clues from nearly everyone in attendance. Toward the end of the evening, the crime appeared no closer to being solved, but the cats had amassed a huge amount of information from eaves dropping, and had begun sorting through the clues.

Mo, Georgia, Diana, Edward, Phillip, Mona, Mac, Murphy, Arbor and Syrah were exhausted from sleuthing, but they felt exhilarated at having gleaned such good information from everyone, including from members of the McMinnville PD.

Now all they had to do was dig out the whys and wherefores, and the case could be closed, thanks to all the sleuthing cats.

CINCO DE MEOW

Chapter 22 –

Like a graceful vase, a cat, even when motionless, seems to flow. George F. Will

Standing in the shadows of the winery tasting room was a person few but John had noticed. He had slipped in when the event was at its busiest. Now he busied himself at trying to appear comfortable in his solitude. He did blend in quite well with the circulating crowd, but was reluctant to leave his sequestered table where no one bothered him and he was not prematurely forced to keep conversation with a room full of strangers. Especially since they all seemed to revere Donald Jenkins, and he was a bit afraid he might just blow his top if he heard one more cheesy comment about the dead man.

That idiot, he thought. Imagine that backwards cowboy thinking he knew better than the experts. GMO grain was more quickly grown and you could harvest three times the grain over non-GMO fields, it had a longer shelf life, and no one could discern a difference in taste or quality. Why then, was it so damned important that GMOs be kept out of the market? The Japanese had even severed grain import ties with Oregon when it was discovered that some of the grain they purchased contained GMOs! Didn't they know that progress is good for everyone? In this case, because there was a perception of a problem, he was better off to ignore it and move the supplies on hand as non-GMO product. The public's 'right to know,' indeed! Unfortunately, the huge storage facility in the Seven Oaks area was directly in line with the new bypass project. Although the depot itself would not need to be moved, the traffic patterns into and out of the depot would be changed considerably, and some of the storage areas needed to be relocated for easier access. That would mean accelerated shipping and emptying of the storage bins. And then a few days ago he had received word that the government testers would descend on the warehouse and silos again in short order.

All because Donald Jenkins had alerted someone in an obscure government office somewhere to a fact he had blundered upon. The grain stored in the Seven Oaks facility was almost entirely GMO-enhanced. When peripheral testing had been done several months earlier, much money had changed hands between certain hand-picked inspectors and himself, as part-owner and site manager. Grain was tested alright, but it was directed to be sampled from a particular area of storage which housed a small quantity of non-GMO grain.

Then Donald took it upon himself to send samples of grain and feed that had been delivered to Knightly Ranch to an independent tester. He had only received the results from those tests the evening before his so-called tragic demise.

A demise orchestrated, although perhaps by happenstance, by this same man who stood in the shadows. A man who held nearly one quarter of Western Hay and Grain's lucrative stocks. A man who now needed to empty the Western Hay and Grain warehouse of GMO feed before those inspectors arrived.

He decided he must move around a bit to listen to conversations of people in the room. He needed to know if Donald had provided the results to anyone else, and everyone who might need that information from ranchers to county commissioners, was in the room.

CINCO DE MEOW

Chapter 23 –

The idea of calm exists in a sitting cat. *Jules Reynard*

The Ten cats stood quietly and formed a straight line like offensive line blockers. Their faces were masked with devil-may-care expressions, and not once did any one of them blink. Mona broke the silence as she continued to stare off into the room to the winery's reveling patrons.

I spy a stranger in our midst. That man over there behind the barrels. He's been at the same table for about twenty minutes and has not yet spoken with anyone here.

Well, perhaps he just doesn't know anyone here, suggested Georgia. *He may be hoping someone will engage him in conversation. This is a friendly crowd, but he doesn't seem inclined to move into any of the circles to be included.*

I recognize that man, said Mo. *I only caught a brief glimpse, but he was the driver of the grain truck leaving the Knightly Ranch on the morning Kate and I went to look for Donald. It was a Western Hay and Grain truck, the company we talked about earlier. I wonder what brings him here tonight? Maybe he was a friend of Donald's.*

Or maybe he just likes good wine and good food and wants to get to know some local people, offered Mac.

As they discussed the mysterious stranger, that same man began to move around the room. The cats watched as he introduced himself to as many people as he could reach over the next half hour. As he passed by the cats on his way to one of the exits, the cats, still sitting in their linebacker array, suddenly stiffened and displayed a communal sneer. Their facial expressions were formed in identical manner with the flehmen response.

The flehmen response is how cats direct particles to the vomeronasal organ for analysis.

CINCO DE MEOW

The vomeronasal organ is an olfactory structure located between a cat's hard palate and nasal septum. The vomeronasal organ is used to analyze pheromones, which is an important way cats communicate. Pheromones are needed to keep cats balanced, having a sense of continuity. These cats were responding to some negative pheromones with disquieting odors after taking a deep inhale of whatever they sensed on the stranger.

Anyone looking at the cats would have marveled that all ten could make the same face at the same time. Charles, however, spotted the display, and suspected that if all ten cats were united in their senses, the cats were probably on to something. Charles had never dismissed a cat's sense of danger. At the very least, he knew the cats had collectively sensed unpleasant company or an inharmonious deed.

Charles made a note of the stranger who had just passed by the cats and who was headed toward the front exit. He did not recognize the man. Because the man had not presented any outward signs of threat and had been cordial to the people he had spoken with, Charles had nothing to go on, and decided not to pursue at this time his suspicions, which were, after all, based upon his perception of ten cats' intuitions. He would, however, begin speaking with those with whom the stranger had spoken that evening, in the hopes of learning something about the man and perhaps his reasons for being at the event.

CINCO DE MEOW

Chapter 24 –

No amount of time can erase the memory of a good cat, and no amount of masking tape can ever totally remove his fur from your couch. Leo Dworken

Charles had seen the stranger speak with Kate briefly, so he promptly headed toward Kate to sound her out first. He knew her intuition was tantamount to the cats' and if anyone could sense something was off, it was Kate.

"Well Kate," began Charles, "how are you holding up? I think you've probably spoken with each and every person in attendance here tonight."

"I admit I'm beginning to tire," said Kate. "But everyone here is so energized, I can't even think about winding up the event. I am aware of the lateness of the hour, Charles, and I'll make sure we escort everyone to the doors by midnight. I've already sent the Townsley group out to the limo. They live close and were dropped off here by one of their cousins who owns a van. Unfortunately, the van is unavailable for a late-night pick-up. I'm so glad people are conscious of the danger of drinking and driving."

"I've been keeping a watchful eye on our guests, as well," replied Charles. "They are a good group and I've not noticed anyone abusing tasting privileges, and most guests have limited themselves to one or two glasses of wine over the course of the evening. Besides, they all know I'm here and aware, as well as is half the McMinnville PD. Still, I'll make sure to monitor everyone as they leave for their own safety. At guests' requests, we have set up a breathalyzer station at the front door, so anyone who doubts their sobriety, can verify that before they get behind the wheel. Better to be safe than sorry, especially when we're providing transportation for anyone needing it.

"Kate, I really wanted to talk to you about a conversation you had with a gentleman who just left because I saw you speaking with him. Had you met him before and did he say what his business was here?"

"No, although I swear he looks familiar, I've never met the man before," answered Kate. "He introduced himself as Duke Loma. He told me he was in a new partnership with three other owners of Western Hay and Grain, and that he was interested in meeting some of Western's clients and generally getting to know people around here."

"Did he say anything about where he is based?" queried Charles.

"He did mention that he considered his home base in Idaho until he can find permanent residence in the area. He also stated that, although he was managing the site, he had been helping out driving the delivery trucks since they had not yet been able to fill those positions. By the way, Charles, Mr. Loma asked if I knew of anyone who would be interested in driving for Western. Do you think that the new owners are trying to generate more jobs in the area?"

"It's too early to tell, Kate," responded Charles. "They've assumed deliveries to all of the ranchers in the area previously served by West Coast. I did hear from George that when the new management came on board and changed the name to Western Hay and Grain, some of the long-time employees decided to take advantage of the previous owner's offer to retire early with a pension. Others just moved on to other jobs, I suppose. That left quite a few positions unfilled, so it's logical that the new management would need to fill in until they can hire new staff."

"Mr. Loma did ask me a strange question," confided Kate. "He asked if I had heard whether construction would be moved up on the bypass project. He indicated that things were in a state of flux at Western Grain because there would be new entrances and exits requiring some grain storage relocation and major security fencing enhancements because of the proposed traffic patterns. I don't think he was too pleased that the project was moving along at the speed it seems to be moving now. I, for one, am only too happy that the project is finally going forward, and I would have assumed that ample time was given in the contract for the new owners to comply with the new standards. It's certainly no secret."

"That's something I'll need to discuss with George," said Charles. "It may be that the new owners didn't thoroughly vet the impact of the bypass project on the grain depot. From my perspective, though, I would think they'd be happy to have their highway access more organized, and it certainly will be a safer corridor for the grain trucks and for other drivers."

"Well, he seemed nice enough, Charles," said Kate, "but he wasn't interested in talking very long. He seemed anxious to keep moving. Do you think I may have offended him in some way?"

"No, I don't think so, Kate," laughed Charles. "First of all, I've not known you to offend anyone, and my sense of Duke Loma is that he is trying to get as much information in as short a time period as possible. I observed that he made a beeline for George when he finished speaking with you. And George is next on my list to speak to. It also appears that Mr. Loma knew exactly who George was, and would know that most, if not all information related to the bypass, could be gained through George. I'll let you know if I find out anything pertinent, so you can tend to your guests and I'll tend to the stranger."

Chapter 25 –

Most beds sleep up to six cats. Ten cats without the owner.
Stephen Baker

George was attempting to corral Mona, Mac and Murphy to shuttle them home when Charles approached him about Duke Loma. George, however, was very preoccupied with herding his cats, so Charles told George he'd call him in the morning. George was grateful, as he'd no sooner managed setting the three in a spearhead to the door than Mona was off like a shot back into the venue. George was truly flustered, but perhaps no more so than the cats, who had enjoyed their evening with their friends, the first in a very long time that had brought them all together again. As George ushered Mac and Murphy into their respective carriers, Kate brought up the rear holding the elusive Mona in her arms. Mona appeared resigned to the fate awaiting her in the SUV and riding home in the carrier, so she nestled against Kate and just accepted it.

Georgia and Rebecca had left the event earlier, as Rebecca didn't like to leave Lawrence, Jr. for too long. As soon as they arrived home, Rebecca bundled him up and she and Georgia took their wonderful child care attendants (babysitters), Pippa and Beatrice home. All through the ride to the Kensington house, little Junior was held and coddled and cooed at, but nothing could keep him from sleeping like a stone.

James pulled The Spay Station up to the side entrance, and left the engine running to warm up the inside for the cats. He, too, had to do a little feline chasing, as Arbor and Syrah had been enjoying their time with their feline friends and did not want to leave. It seemed the two cats had radar, or at least eyes in the back of their heads. As soon as James approached them, and as a veterinarian he knew how to execute a stealthy approach, the two ran in opposite directions, thereby diluting the chance of a catch.

Arbor and Syrah

Diana, Edward and Phillip marched with tails held high to Elizabeth's car when she beckoned them. Better to pick your battles, they thought, and they certainly wanted to conserve all their strength to put the finishing touches on their soft sell campaign to place little Victoria with Phillip. They began the 'mind deluge' as soon as Elizabeth started the car.

Elizabeth couldn't help thinking about Victoria as she dropped Diana and Edward off at the Kensington's home. She knew that Phillip would immediately bemoan his solitary confinement. Sure enough, no sooner had his two friends been ushered to the waiting arms of Pippa and Beatrice, than Phillip began his pitiful crying. Well, that settles it, thought Elizabeth. I'll call Olivia in the morning to see if Victoria can at least have a play date with Phillip. And I'll discuss my thoughts about putting the two of them together permanently for company – and for my enjoyment, too. It's too bad that Lady, Señor, Winston and Squeaks couldn't attend to see the whole gang, she thought, but they have each other, and someone had to stay with Olivia and Andrew to console them tonight.

Kate, Charles, John, Mary and William tidied up the tasting room a bit, but John had hired a cleaning service to come in the morning to finish the job. Besides, he was feeling drained from battling his blasted cold and the medicine seemed to be wearing thin. The group was euphoric, though, because the evening had gone so well. Mo had stayed close to her mum after her friends' departures. She was pleased because they had learned much about current events in the area, and they would soon begin piecing clues together to bring Donald's killer to justice.

At the same time, they would all begin the short trek to the Memorial Day Weekend event.

In the back of his pickup, the man had stowed an arsenal of weapons, mostly for hunting but also, in his mind, for self-defense. He was as much a redneck as he was a dyed-in-the-wool radical, as he was a supporter of secretly introducing GMO products to the region. How funny is that? he thought. I can wear three faces at the same time, and these hicks don't recognize me in any of them. Well, soon they will see all my personas in the form of my accomplishments. What the heck, he thought. I'll enjoy a belly laugh – out loud – as I'm the only audience that matters anyway! He laughed and laughed and bent over the wheel in glee.

He suddenly sobered. Now, if I could just locate my hunting knife. I miss that thing.

Such a sharp blade and just the right length to do any job. Well, he would go back to the Knightly Ranch tomorrow and get it back. He knew just about where he must have dropped it.

As Duke Loma drove off into the night, he was still chuckling to himself at the stupidity of the locals.

CINCO DE MEOW

Chapter 26 –

Of all the animals, he alone attains to the Contemplative Life. Andrew Lang

     The following day brought sunshine sparkling off the early misty fog in the valley. George King, who was also the editor of the local newspaper, the *Jory Hills Times*, published a wonderful editorial about the winery and Yamhill Valley's pinot noir wines in general. He had actually worked on the editorial for several weeks. As it happened, the prior evening's event coincided with a recent accolade in *Wine Aficionado*, the wine industry's leading publication.

CINCO DE MEOW

OREGON PINOT NOIR IS NATION'S BEST
Editorial Contributor George King

Wine Aficionado heaped lavish praise on the state in its latest issue, glowingly pronouncing that Oregon is now second-to-none in this country when it comes to its signature wine grape. Talk about getting crushed – Oregon blew California off the map when it comes to producing world-class *Pinot Noir*.

The timing of the article's acclaim came at the precise moment Oregon winemakers are seizing the opportunity to create national wine-tourism destinations in a raft of new tasting rooms scattered throughout Yamhill, Polk and Marion counties. And on the eve, no less, of the Memorial Day wine-tasting weekend, one of the biggest sales and winery touring events of the year.

In its desire to guarantee a more intimate experience for visitors, the winery at Kats Jory Hills Estate Vineyard will open a new 5,000-square-foot tasting room replete with ancillary areas where it can host small groups for personalized tastings. That concept was tested at the *Cinco de Mayo* event hosted last evening by the winery. Raves and accolades came from all in attendance, not only for the stellar wines they enjoyed, but for the facility itself.

"In terms of worldwide wine production, we're just a pin prick here," offered William Kent, Kats' Jory Hills Estate winemaker. "There's just not much to begin with. Because of that, consumers can be thankful the state doesn't have to rely on sheer quantity for success. Given that Oregon produces only about one percent of all wine made in the country, quantity is simply not there."

So the message of quality will be the one vintners will repeat all Memorial Day weekend, as thousands of wine lovers fan out not only across the northern Willamette Valley, but also in other winegrowing areas of the state. Those include the Columbia Gorge, southern parts of the valley and the Rogue and Umpqua valleys in southern Oregon.

"We want to make a statement," contributed John Ferguson, Kats Jory Hills Estate Vineyard and Winery owner. "We are out to offer one of the best wine country experiences you'll have on the West Coast. And we have several delightful B&Bs just steps away, one to which I have bragging rights, *Kats English Bed and Breakfast*, with my lovely daughter, Kate as its hostess and proprietor. So welcome to Wine Country! You'll be treated like royalty and are guaranteed to enjoy our famous pinot noirs!"

Sounds like a great way to spend Memorial Day Weekend. See you there!

Kate and John, as well as William Kent and all the other employees and volunteers at Kats Jory Hills Estate Winery were thrilled with George's editorial, as well as with the *Wine Aficionado*'s stamp of approval. Already they were planning ahead to the Memorial Day Weekend extravaganza. They had gathered at Kats Jory Hills Estate Winery this morning not only to help with the clean-up from last evening, but to begin arranging for the Memorial Day Weekend festivities.

Mo was amused watching the spectacle. She was glad she didn't have the same responsibilities as her two-legged friends.

163

CINCO DE MEOW

Later this morning, she would stop in at the shelter to settle any new arrivals, and to congratulate several residents who were going to forever homes. She knew that seven cats had found loving homes over the weekend. Kate always got so excited when any of the shelter cats found a second chance for loves of their lives, and Kate had gotten her update early that morning from the shelter.

Mo would also make sure that Kate hooked her up with Mona, Mac and Murphy, as well as with Georgia so they could formulate a plan to expose Donald's killer. No time like the present, and the longer they waited, the more chance he had to disappear. They also needed to spread the word to Lady and Señor, as well as to Squeaker and Winston. Of course, Arbor and Syrah, and Diana, Edward and Phillip had prior commitments to honor today, but they were already up to speed on the events of the previous night and they, too, thought they knew exactly who the slayer was. Yes, it would be a red letter day and the cats looked forward to entertaining Justice in the matter.

And so, the cleaning progressed speedily and the humans chatted vigorously. Only the unsolved crime dampened the group's spirits as they plunged in with the professional cleaners to put the tasting room back in order.

CINCO DE MEOW

Chapter 27 –

Way down deep, we're all motivated by the same urges.
Cats have the courage to live by them. *Jim Davis*

Shortly after reading George's editorial and consuming three cups of very black coffee, Elizabeth could wait no longer to call Olivia to pave the way for Victoria Kitty to live with her and Phillip.

"Phillip is so lonely," moaned Elizabeth to Olivia over the phone. "Do you think we could arrange a play date between the two? It would be such a relief if Phillip could enjoy company all day long and especially when I'm out of the house. And in the long term, don't you think Victoria would benefit from living with us?"

"Oh, I do believe they would be much happier together," replied Olivia who had long been expecting this or a similar call. "In fact, I was thinking about Victoria's relative seclusion here just this morning and I do think she would adore Phillip and enjoy new surroundings with her friend."

Victoria

"That settles it!" cried Elizabeth, so happy that both she and Olivia were on the same page regarding the welfare of the two cats. "I'll drop by this morning and pick her up. I'll bring Phillip with me and the two can begin to 'sniff and socialize' in the car during the trip home. Oh, I'm so excited for Phillip, the lonely little guy. He has so needed company and Victoria is just perfect! She will be so welcome here and she will become my second 'child,' just as Phillip is my first 'child'."

After reading the newspaper and eating a very large breakfast, Charles pulled out his phone and called George. He intended fully to continue the conversation he attempted to complete last evening when George had become distracted by those rascal kitties.

"Good morning, George! Are you settled in with your cats this morning?" Charles asked when George answered on the first ring. "Those little angels seemed to have minds of their own last evening, probably giddy from their romping all over the winery last night."

CINCO DE MEOW

"Well, I'll say they gave me a run for my money," confessed George. "But you know I wouldn't have it any other way, Charles."

"Yes, so I see," said Charles. "They are your babies. And I enjoyed the editorial you ran in *The Jory Hills Times* this morning. Wonderful exposure for wineries in the area, and these local vintners appreciate your support. But I'm also calling to see if you would grant me a few minutes of your valuable time to talk with me about Duke Loma."

"I have to tell you," mused George, "that I would suspect Duke Loma of shady activity if for no other reason than last evening he was pointedly asking questions no normal person would care about. And I don't know the man from Adam. Imagine, at a social event, all he wanted to discuss was poor Donald's demise and why it was so important that non-GMO products be sold in Oregon! Well, I'm doing an investigative piece on Western Grain, and since he's an integral part of that enterprise, I'll do some investigating into Duke as well."

"Now George, we've had this discussion before," chuckled Charles. "Please leave the criminal investigations to me, if you don't mind. I know you are a Cracker Jack reporter, and your writing skills are legendary, but I'm concerned you might dig up something that would help the investigation, only to have any evidence deemed inadmissible because it wasn't properly processed and channeled. You have enough to do with all the irons you have in the fire: you're chief reporter and editor of the *Jory Hills Times*, you're a Yamhill County Commissioner, and your biggest responsibility is being a loving husband, as well as a 'father' to those cats."

"I hear what you're saying, Charles," replied George. "You know I won't interfere with a criminal investigation, especially when the best – meaning you, Charles – is leading the review. But I know from my cursory inquiries at Western Grain that Duke Loma is not at all well-received at the company. In fact, he has ruffled quite a few feathers with the more established members of his team, the other owners and the Board of Directors as well."

"Thanks, George," said Charles. "I know I can always count on your professional manner to save the day. Would you keep me updated with reports from the Western Grain staff you're interviewing?"

"Of course, Charles," replied George. "I hope to wrap up my review this afternoon – as commissioner and as an editor – of Western Hay and Grain's treatment of possible GMO contamination. I'll let you know if they reveal anything new. Meanwhile, I need to head over to the newspaper to draft the bones of the editorial for the paper tomorrow."

"I'll speak with you later, George," said Charles as he finished his coffee. "We need to complete this investigation before the trail becomes cold."

Mona, Mac and Murphy sat in the corner behind the couch just as still as stones. They didn't want to move or attract any attention until George had finished his conversation. Hazzah! They had gleaned some very important information about Duke Loma, and they couldn't wait to share it with Mo, and hopefully with Georgia, too. They'd have this crime solved in no time!

The truck containing hay from Western Hay and Grain pulled into the Knightly Ranch driveway. Duke Loma steered the rig down the gravel road while he thought about the real reason for his visit today. He needed to find that lost knife, and he knew just where to look.

He pulled the truck into the covered storage area, and unloaded several bales of hay. Andrew Knightly had not ordered more grain or hay, but Duke knew he could explain his presence by lying through his teeth. If anyone should ask why he was here, he'd just say that he had inadvertently shorted the ranch of 10 bales of hay on his previous delivery, that he had just realized it when doing inventory, and that he wanted to make good on the order.

Duke looked around but didn't see anyone in his vicinity, so he walked slowly over to an ancient large oak tree near the tractor barn. He began searching in that area for his knife, and it wasn't long before he found it under a fallen branch. Duke couldn't believe his luck that the police hadn't searched this area, but then, why would they? Donald's body was found clear out in the field and there was nothing to indicate that anyone had been near this barn on the morning of Donald's unseemly demise.

The knife appeared to have dried blood on its hilt as well as on its blade. Duke immediately wrapped the knife in his handkerchief, placed it carefully in the pocket of his jacket and turned to try and make an undetected return to his truck.

To Duke's dismay, Andrew was standing by the truck as he approached, and the man didn't look at all happy.

"May I ask ye who ordered more hay for the ranch?" queried Andrew as he looked around Duke's truck.

"Sorry, Mr. Knightly," grinned Duke. "I realized only this morning that your last delivery was 10 bales shy of your order, so I thought I'd bring these by."

"Well, I appreciate that, but what were ye doing over by the tractor barn? No bales are stored over there. We have sensitive and skittish horses on this ranch, and they don't take kindly to people poking around."

"I just thought I'd try to find someone to report the delivery to before I headed out," retorted Duke. "Didn't think it would be an issue."

"Well, I'd appreciate if ye would let us know before ye just drop in at the ranch, Duke," admonished Andrew. "As I said, these horses are high strung and they tend to sense strangers as dangers.

"Will do," groused Duke. "Although next time maybe I'll rethink making good on an under-filled order. Or maybe Western could be cutting off your deliveries completely."

With that, Duke climbed into his truck and took off down the gravel road. And just for good measure, he spun his tires and spewed gravel back toward the spot where Andrew was standing.

CINCO DE MEOW

Chapter 28 –

God is really only another artist. He invented the giraffe, the elephant and the cat. He has no real style. He just goes on trying other things. *Pablo Picasso*

After Duke left the ranch, Andrew called Charles to convey the details of Duke's visit. He reported to Charles that Duke had been sleuthing around the tractor barn, and was seen by one of his crew lifting up a tree branch out under the old oak. More importantly, one of the ranch hands, Jaime, reported that Duke appeared to have found something that he took away with him. Jaime could not see what it was the Duke found, but he told Andrew that it was a small object.

"I do appreciate your report," Charles said as he took notes. "I'll send a deputy over shortly. If Loma removed something from your property, perhaps he neglected to remove residue, or he might even have left another kind of signature out there."

"My thoughts exactly, Charles," replied Andrew. "Aye, the guy gives me the wee-willies, and when I questioned his actions this morning, he became very defensive. He also threatened to cut off grain supplies to the ranch, and he sprayed me with gravel as he stormed his truck off the place. I'll be speaking with the other Western Grain owners today about that threat. I could only think the worst of that sneaky Loma, and good riddance to him!"

Mo "thought" to Kate that it was urgent to visit with Georgia, Mona, Mac and Murphy, and so Kate – shaking her head at the unexpected idea that had come into her mind just at that moment – picked up Georgia from Rebecca's house, and dropped the two off at George's house. Actually, the visit was appropriately timed as Kate had wanted to thank George for his glowing editorial. She had received several phone calls from friends and neighbors just this morning, even before she checked in with the shelter, and they all wanted to congratulate her on the success of the winery and the B&B.

As soon as the cats stopped in front of George's house, they leaped from the Mini and stormed the back porch where Mona, Mac and Murphy were anxiously waiting.

Mo! Georgia! screeched Mac. *Wait until you hear what we overheard about Duke Loma!*

What? You found something that will help us solve Donald's murder? cried Georgia, who was literally skipping on her four paws.

Well, replied Mona with a much calmer demeanor than her offspring, *we did overhear George speaking with Charles, and we think Duke would have had a motive to kill Donald. What if Donald knew that Duke was trying to sneak GMO grain into everyone's non-GMO coffers? What if Donald threatened to expose Duke to Andrew, or to the police? That would certainly be motive for murder!*

I think you're on to something! cried Mo. *I'll be sending this information to Kate as soon as we formulate a plan to get Charles to bring Duke in for questioning. Kate can't possibly know where the information is coming from, and certainly, Charles wouldn't just arrest Duke on Kate's hunch.*

We can't run him down ourselves, said Georgia. *Let's put our heads together and THINK – ARREST DUKE!*

Kate was sitting in George's parlour when a thought occurred to her.

"I have had the most peculiar urges this morning, George," said Kate shaking her head. "I just *had* to bring the cats by to visit. I just *had* to speak with you about Duke Loma, and now I just *have* to tell you I think Charles should arrest, or at least question, the man! I apologize for sounding demanding or off the wall, but I can't seem to keep my nose out of Donald's death investigation."

"I have to say, Kate," replied George with a twinkle in his eye, "I've had the same uncontrollable urges lately. And seemingly always when the cats are around. Look at them! All five of them sitting there and staring at us like we're bugs!"

Kate chuckled and shook her head again, as she well knew that feeling. "George, whatever else we do today, we really need to convince Charles that Duke is up to something, and perhaps has played a starring role in this case. Yes, I think Duke Loma could be our killer."

"Well, Kate," George said as he pulled his eyes away from the cats, "I've already confided my suspicions of Duke to Charles, and I relayed what Donald told me and why I think it is important. Most of all, I wanted Charles to know that Duke is obviously nervous and is casting about for ways to throw us off the investigation."

"I think it's about time I rounded up my two charges and stopped by the shelter," said Kate as she fished in her pack for the car keys. "I'll stop by the McMinnville PD to speak with Charles. I do hope he has had some luck with his interviews. Someone at that ranch must have seen something that morning. Come on, Mo, Georgia! Off to the Mini. We'll visit with Mona, Mac and Murphy again very soon."

Chapter 29 –

Ignorant people think it's the noise which fighting cats make that is so aggravating, but it ain't so; it's the sickening grammar they use. *Mark Twain*, A Tramp Abroad

Charles Beltz closed and locked the drawers to his desk at the McMinnville Police Department. He had just hung up from another call to Andrew Knightly, and he was pleased yet dismayed with the information Andrew had given him. Andrew had reiterated that Duke threatened him with denying Knightly Ranch feed for the horses, and also that the man had a trigger temper.

CINCO DE MEOW

Andrew had also told Charles that he believed that one or more of his ranch hands must have witnessed something on the morning Donald was killed because they were all acting strangely distant and unnaturally somber. 'Strangely,' to the Scotsman included acts such as Jaime, Juan and Paco speaking to each other only in Spanish so that anyone who might overhear their conversation would not understand what they were saying. Andrew also thought that Paco, especially, had been nervous and irritable. All of these actions were very much unlike the three ranch hands. Andrew had come upon Jaime and Paco in the tractor barn where they appeared to be in a heated argument. As soon as they spotted Andrew, they stopped their bellicose behavior and greeted him normally. But they left in a hurry, and Andrew reportedly heard Paco tell Jaime as they closed the barn door that "it's not your family that is in danger, so how can you tell me what to do?"

Charles left the police department and drove in a squad car to the Knightly Ranch. Andrew greeted him warmly, and invited Charles into the house, where Paco was waiting in the kitchen at the table.

"Good morning, Paco," Charles greeted the ranch hand with a handshake. "I hope I haven't taken you away from some very pressing duties here at the ranch, and I promise I'll only take a half hour of your time."

At the mention of 'half hour,' Paco winced. A half hour could be a lifetime if he said the wrong thing or if he broke down and said the right thing. Paco waited patiently for Charles to begin the interview. It seemed that his whole life hung on the ensuing moments.

"I'll brew up some coffee, gents," said Andrew as he scurried to the far end of the kitchen to make the brew.

"Paco, I have the feeling you know more than you're telling me about Donald's death," began Charles. "But I also believe that a man of your integrity must have a good reason for not telling me everything you know. I want to assure you that no harm will come to you if you didn't play any part in Donald's death, and you'll have the full protection of the department if you are concerned for your safety."

"Señor, it is not for my own safety that I would be concerned," said Paco with downcast eyes. "I am concerned for my family in Mexico. I have arranged to bring my wife and my two sons to Oregon next fall, and I am now worried that they will be in danger here. It has taken me many years to save enough to bring them here, where their lives should be much better. Now, I wonder if they are not better off staying in Nuevo Leon."

"Paco," Charles said as he placed his hand on Paco's shoulder, "if someone has threatened you or your family, you need to tell me. As I said, the department can protect you now, and if whoever threatened you is 'put away' they can't harm your family when they arrive in September. Please tell me what you know about Donald's death."

"Oh Señor, I am so sorry I did not come forward right away," moaned Paco. "I woke up early on that morning, and went to the barns to get a head start on the day's chores. I saw Donald, and he waved to me. I was working in the barn, but I did see a man walking down the road to the ranch. I was very busy with my work and I did not think he saw me. He found Donald and they started shouting. I saw him and Donald go out into the field. I saw the two men wrestling with a knife, and I saw Donald fall. I only saw the other man come back."

"What happened next, Paco?" asked Charles who wrote down Paco's statement as they sat together in the kitchen. Andrew had placed steaming cups of coffee in front of both men, and had moved back to the sink to begin washing some pots that had been soaking.

"I was wrong thinking that the man did not see me. He came toward me with the knife in his hand. He said it was an accident, that Donald pushed him first and that he drew his knife to defend himself against Donald. He told me, 'I cannot be associated in any way with Jenkins' death. It was an accident, but the police will never believe me. If you tell them what you saw, they will arrest me and jail me or worse. So I tell you this: if you tell the police what you saw here today, I will not only kill you, I will hunt down your family and kill them, too.' Oh, Lieutenant Beltz, because he was evil enough to threaten me and my family I do not believe that he did not come here to kill Donald. I do not care about my safety, but he can hurt my family and they are everything to me!"

"What happened to the knife, Paco," queried Charles who was trying with his voice to calm Paco down so he didn't freeze up in front of him or lose the momentum of his story. "You said he came toward you with the knife. Do you know where the knife is now?"

"No, I do not, Señor Beltz. After he threatened me, he told me to stay in the barn because he would be watching. He left through the big doors and I saw him pass the oak tree and go into the vineyard."

"Now, Paco," said Charles sternly, "I'm going to ask you the man's name, and if you know it, you must tell me. It's the only way I can protect you and your family."

"It was Duke Loma," replied Paco with tears rolling down his cheeks. "He is the man who brings the hay and grain to us. He came back later that morning in the hay truck to make a delivery and to warn me again. He was looking around the barns, but he finished unloading the hay just before Miss Kate got here. They passed each other on the road coming into the ranch."

"Paco, you've been more than helpful," said Charles quietly. "I'm going to ask you to come with me to the station so you can give a recorded statement to the detectives. Are you willing to do that so that we can arrest Loma? He will receive a fair trial, and if Donald's death was an accident, that will come out. I think

Loma probably came back to the ranch with the hay that morning to look for his knife, but he didn't have time to find it. Andrew spotted Loma here a while ago, and when questioned, he said he was delivering more hay. Andrew thought he was lying, and Jaime saw Loma pick something up near the oak tree by the tractor barn and take it with him. I've got a team of forensic experts on its way here now to see what they can find in the area. The lab results from the blood that we sent in from the scene matched only Donald's, and I predict there will be Donald's blood residue near that oak tree, as well."

Andrew, who had stayed busy while Charles and Paco were talking, refilled the two cups of coffee on the table. Paco thanked him profusely, as he was badly shaken. The two gulped the new brew, and Charles led Paco to his car after explaining to Andrew why they were leaving. Andrew looked relieved, and whispered to Paco that he was proud of him for having given information to Charles even though he was afraid.

"Paco," said Andrew, "ye can be assured that yer job here is secure, and no one will come here to harm ye or yer family when they arrive. Ye did a bonny thing, and I'm sure Charles will have ye back here in a few hours. I hope ye will accept my invitation to dinner this evening so we can discuss plans for yer family's living arrangements when they arrive. I want them to be comfortable and I want ye to be close by so ye won't have far to travel to come to the ranch. I think of ye as family, and I'm honored that ye trusted Charles and I enough to tell us what ye saw, even after such a heinous threat from Loma."

Paco waved to Andrew as Charles drove off to McMinnville with Paco in the passenger seat. Paco also hoped that these men knew how excruciating it had been for him to reveal the truth when the safety of his family was in the balance. He was proud to be a citizen, and equally proud that he would have a part in bringing Donald's killer to justice.

CINCO DE MEOW

Chapter 30 –

Of all domestic animals the cat is the most expressive. His face is capable of showing a wide range of expressions. His tail is a mirror of his mind. His gracefulness is surpassed only by his agility. And, along with all these, he has a sense of humor. *Walter Chandoha*

Charles checked Paco in at the station, and assured the man that he was not in trouble for failing to tell his story earlier, that he knew Paco was afraid after his family had been threatened. He advised Paco that two detectives would be interviewing him, and that his statement would be recorded. Charles did his best to make Paco comfortable, but he understood that many people are naturally nervous being questioned, especially in a police station. He closed the door to the interview room, and set off to see Kate as he had promised to do earlier.

Duke decided to pay George a visit – with the express purpose of dissuading him from publishing the editorial about the possible GMO contamination.

"It's against my better judgment to let you into my home," snapped George as he stood at the front door looking at the man. "If you have something to say or perhaps to *confess*, you should make tracks to the McMinnville PD, Loma."

"Now George," smiled Duke unconvincingly, "I wouldn't dream of depriving you of first-hand knowledge. I don't know to what you are referring, but I have bigger fish to fry today. I do hope you won't be riling the locals up about possible GMOs in their food. I have it on good authority that the problem doesn't exist in the Yamhill Valley."

"You and I both know that isn't true," seethed George as he stood blocking Duke's entry into his house. "If what I suspect is true, your grain operation could be closed down, and you will be out of work. And that's the least of your worries. Maybe time to go back to Idaho."

"I like it here," retorted Duke as he tried to move past George. Then he spied the cats sitting in the hallway behind George. "It'd be too bad if something happened to those cats. They might fare better if you backed off this crusade of yours and just let things be."

"That does it, Loma," shouted George. "Take your carcass off my property. If something happened to my cats, I would know exactly where to look for the culprit!"

Duke strode down George's front steps to his car, but turned back to George as he opened the driver's door. "Don't say I didn't warn you, King. I'll sue you for every penny you ever thought of having if you accuse me or Western Grain of wrongdoing. And those cats would just be collateral damage."

Duke roared off down the street, leaving George a bit shaken inside his front door. "Don't you worry your little heads," George cooed to the kitties who were looking quite spooked. "That man won't have the chance to get near my babies, and I'm going to the study to finish that editorial right now. It'll be in tomorrow morning's edition."

CINCO DE MEOW

The cats for their part were not just spooked: they were enraged! How dare that man threaten their da' and them, too! They would 'make' George pick up the phone and call Charles to relay the events that had transpired.

Which is exactly what George started to do, but he first called Kate to get her take on the conversation before he called the police. Kate, too, was furious when she heard the threats, and of course, Mo overheard the conversation and powered herself to full telepathy mode.

Mum, you must report this to Charles immediately. George may not wish to appear frightened, but he most certainly is, and he's most concerned for Mona, Mac and Murphy!

As luck would have it, Charles arrived at Kate's cottage at just that moment, and Kate relayed to Charles what had taken place at George's house.

"Well, that does it," sighed Charles in disgust. "I was going to give Duke a courtesy call and ask him to come to the station for a chat. Now I'll ask George to come on down, too, and file a complaint. I'm hoping I can get a subpoena to search Loma's house. My forensic folks rushed to the ranch, found dried blood near the oak tree and sent it in for an emergency lab test. We need to find the knife that killed Donald; and if I were a betting man, I'd bet my bottom dollar it is hidden somewhere around Loma's house."

CINCO DE MEOW

Chapter 31 –

Who can believe there is no soul behind those luminous eyes! *Theophile Gautier*

Corruption is like a lily – brush against it, however, lightly, and some of the pollen smears on you. Therefore, choose your friends wisely. Concern yourself more with that person's character than his resume. This gets back to: trust your instincts. *Unknown*

From the moment Charles heard Paco's eyewitness account of the events on the morning of Donald's death, compounded by Duke's threat to Paco and to George, the case at the McMinnville PD was accelerated to a fast pace.

Charles called in the threats to the station and ordered that two detectives locate Duke Loma and bring him in for questioning. He also advised George King to come in to file a complaint against Duke. Charles' third call was to the prosecuting attorney, who called Judge Collins, who agreed with both Charles' and the DA's assessments, and signed the search warrant, which opened the way for the search of Duke Loma's property, including his vehicles.

Duke arrived at the station in a squad car and was immediately assigned to the two detectives who brought him in, and they commenced questioning him in an interview room. Duke vehemently denied having anything to do with killing Donald Jenkins, and refused to sit still and answer questions. He continually interrupted every question with threats to sue the McMinnville Police Department, the Commissioners and Charles personally. He blamed the county for unnecessarily condemning GMO grain as deficient and somehow dangerous, and he rounded out the count by claiming defamation of character for being accused of any wrongdoing. He intimated that all of the owners at Western Hay and Grain knew the facts about GMOs, that they would have no objection to selling GMO grain, and that they would all be aware of GMO grain at the warehouses, if that, in fact, proved to be the case.

Meanwhile, the police searched Duke's house and vehicle, and located a knife wrapped in a handkerchief and wedged between the seats of his pick-up. They also located several guns and rifles that, although legally permitted, were thought to be of excessive number and brawn for hunting or for self-defense.

Paco had completed giving his statement and was speaking with Charles at the station, when he spied Duke Loma being escorted to an interrogation room. Although Duke couldn't see Paco, the poor man went to pieces and asked Charles again for protection for his family. At that, Charles assured Paco that he and his family would be safe from harm.

The forensics folks who had rushed to the scene had accelerated the blood testing on the knife, and the lab produced the results post haste. The blood found on the knife proved to be that of Donald Jenkins. Charles had received that report by phone from the lab just prior to calling the DA's office, and he knew that at the very least, Duke would be formally arrested and stand trial for killing Donald. He would be under constant scrutiny and if he was released on bail, the police would monitor his moves and if necessary, would assign a patrol to protect anyone Duke had threatened.

Charles poked his head into the interrogation room, and advised the detectives and Duke about the forensics report they had received and asked the detectives to read Loma his Rights again.

Duke, now caught in the evidence paradox, backtracked and recanted his previous story. He spent the next few hours admitting that he killed Donald, but claimed that it was accidental, that he was defending himself, and that he'd had no intention of killing Donald on the morning of his death.

For the McMinnville PD, for Charles, for Paco and George and the rest of the community (including the Cats), it was a day of reckoning and relief. The man who killed Donald was under arrest, and now it would be up to a judge and jury to decide whether Loma had murdered Donald or whether Donald's death was accidental or a result of self-defense. The community had faith in the judicial system and would await whatever outcome came to pass.

Chapter 32 –

Cats are a mysterious kind of folk. There is more passing in their minds than we are aware of. Sir Walter Scott

Having completed interviews with Western Grain's co-owners – with the exception of Duke Loma – George King published his probing editorial which provided a scathing view of Western Feed and Grain and its role in introducing GMO grain to unaware ranchers locally. He personally didn't feel that the other owners were aware of the tainted grain, but as with any other problem, the buck stopped at the bottom line – it was the duty of the other three owners to ride herd on Duke. Since they

198

failed in that, they had to accept responsibility for Duke's actions.

George's editorial revealed that although the grain at Western had been tested, the sample the inspector was provided came from a small stockpile of grain that was non-GMO. And of course it passed the test. He had interviewed Andrew and the third-party inspector who had received Donald's grain sample, and published their stories that grain delivered to Andrew was genetically modified – and that Andrew did not know about the modification nor had he chosen to feed his horses GMO hay and grain.

One of the inspectors from the county who passed the first GMO grain sample was interviewed, and denied any payoff or bribe to pass the sample, and he also testified that Duke had directed him to the location of the sample he had subsequently taken. Questions remained, though, as to why the inspector would acquiesce to such a limited sample, when the job of the county was to verify that *all* the grain was GMO-free.

George had faith that with the expert investigative skills of the McMinnville PD, led of course by Charles Beltz, added to the solidarity of the community on this issue, the question of whether GMOs were being silently sold to an unsuspecting public would be answered quickly.

And the community could thank Donald Jenkins for his tenacity in digging out the truth, a truth for which he exchanged his life.

The three co-owners could answer the challenge made in George's editorial – or not. As Charles had promised to begin a formal investigation, George didn't think it would take too much time to clear the air. The courts would also need to decide if Duke masterminded the sale of GMO grain and if the other partners truly were unaware of the deception.

For their part, the other partners chose to leave Duke Loma in jail to make his own bail.

CINCO DE MEOW

Chapter 33 –

Even overweight cats instinctively know the cardinal rule: when fat, arrange yourself in slim poses. *John Weitz*

Memorial Weekend came and went. The vineyards and wineries in Yamhill Valley were chock full of locals and tourists who came to taste wine and to buy their favorites.

Kate's B&B had been full with wine aficionados, and she had offered them first choice to a different venue for the occasion. Kate and her father had put together a fantastic Destination Wine Event, which included Oregon wine competition, vintner dinners, Oregon wine university sensory classes, medal celebration and barrel auctions, a wild salmon bake, and a grand tasting affair. The event had been a sell-out and had included other wineries in the area.

John was euphoric, and his bout with the 'bug' had been squelched. He felt much younger than his years, and was hopeful that the joy brought by Kate, his friends and the wine community would continue to give him a long happy life. George, of course, published another editorial to honor the Memorial Day affair. He summarized his editorial by reading portions of the article to Mona, Mac and Murphy.

George sat in the library with the three cats facing him at attention. He chuckled as he selected passages from the editorial to share with the cats. He explained that he wanted to present a different view on wineries, and so he had settled on explaining why wineries were choosing to sell directly to the public (as with Wine Clubs and by the new 'growler' medium), and how direct sales had increased the exposure, income and sustainability of the local wineries.

"Here's a quote from one of your favorite vintners," said Charles to the cats who sat awaiting his comments. They loved story-telling, and George usually entertained them by using them as 'sounding boards' before he published any of his editorials.

> "Selling wine through distribution channels pays the bills," said John Ferguson, owner of Kats Jory Hills Estate Winery. "But it gives you no return on your investment."
>
> John Ferguson is far from alone in joining what some are calling the "arms race" of competing for direct sales in wine country by ramping up facilities for visitors.
>
> "Revenue from tasting rooms is critical, it really is," offered Ferguson. "Providing folks with something interesting to see and enjoy is a huge part of that.
>
> "Toss in a product that's now hailed as the best of its kind in the nation, and wine aficionados throughout the state flocked to us to enjoy their touring on Memorial Day Weekend."

"I have another special quote you might be interested in," George confessed as the cats still stood patiently waiting for more stories. "It concerns all of you and your wonderful friends, and highlights your importance to the community, especially the wine community. Of course, you know you are my family members and I couldn't imagine spending a day without you. But you should know that my friends and the people who visit the area, come to see you, too, and the wineries wouldn't be the same without you."

Highlighting the festivities during the Memorial Weekend Oregon Wine Country Celebration was the presence of numerous 'Wine Cats' at various wineries. Representing Kats Jory Hills Estate Winery was Mo Ferguson who also serves as liaison to Cats Pause Feline Shelter here in Seven Oaks. On loan to Sol Lina Winery and representing Yamhill County and its Commissioners were Mona, Mac and Murphy King, whose most staunch supporter is George King, of the same Commission. Taking the weekend in stride at Cameron Vineyards was Georgia Sherlock, whose generous companions Rebecca and Lawrence, Jr. (Junior) Sherlock graciously shared Georgia's company. Holding down the cat trees at Winderlea Winery were visiting dignitaries Lady, Señor, Squeaker and Winston Knightly, representing the Knightly Ranch and all the horses residing therein. The Knightly Ranch has its own vineyard, of course, but does not have a winery at this stage. Therefore, the Knightly cats were honored to anchor the helm at Winderlea, as the Knightly Vineyard provides some of the wonderful grapes enhancing Winderlea's crush. Local veterinarian James Middleton brought his two felines, Arbor and Syrah to visit with folks in the Bella Vida Winery. From the Kensington household ventured Diana and Edward, who regally held court at Cathedral Ridge, where many visitors told of the cats being the crowning glories to their visits to wine country. Finally, Phillip and Victoria Conley brought much pleasure to the visitors at Erath Winery, bestowing many purrs upon them. All in all, the cat dignitaries were made to feel as royals by the visitors, and in turn, the cats lavished attention and sandpaper kisses on their adoring crowds."

CINCO DE MEOW

The cats cuddled together by the window and accepted the adoration heaped upon them by their wonderful da'. The life of a cat can only be enhanced by a loving human, and they had certainly found theirs in George.

CINCO DE MEOW

Chapter 34 –

I put down my book, *The Meaning of Zen*, and see the cat smiling into her fur as she delicately combs it with her rough pink tongue. Cat, I would lend you this book to study but it appears you have already read it. She looks up and gives me her full gaze. Don't be ridiculous, she purrs, I wrote it. From <u>Miao</u> by *Dilys Laing*

There is no snooze button on a cat who wants breakfast. *Unknown*

Mona, Mac and Murphy sat staring at George King from their perch on the windowsill. They were feeling much more composed than earlier this morning, now that they had sniffed out a rodent in the basement, cornered a bug on the floor and shredded the morning paper, including the report on Donald's alleged murder (which they knew they and their friends alone, had solved), and listened to George's editorial on the Memorial Day Weekend events.

Many in the valley had enjoyed the Memorial Weekend events, as the valley had been bursting with wine tasters with one delicacy in mind: Oregon pinot noir. Now that Donald's killer had been found, George felt relief that the community could move on. And he felt satisfied that Donald would approve.

At Kats English Bed & Breakfast, Kate enjoyed a morning cup of tea in the sunny tearoom, as the guests had all gone out into wine country to begin another day of tasting and sightseeing in the beautiful Yamhill Valley. If he were here, Kate thought, Donald would take solace in the fact that his killer had been apprehended – and that he had his many friends to thank for their persistence in pursuing the motive, and thus, the killer.

Victoria and Phillip were absolutely blissful at Elizabeth's home, now their furr-ever home. They had become inseparable and protective of each other and of Elizabeth. They, too, were happy that things were returning to normal in the valley, and that Donald's killer would stand trial.

Diana and Edward were in their car carriers accompanying Pippa and Beatrice to the Sherlock household. They looked forward to outings when they could visit Georgia. Rebecca had decided to take on several new clients after a short hiatus from her business, so she picked up the vacationing girls and the cats to bring them to her home for the day. She was relieved that she could leave Lawrence, Jr. with the two girls, and her neighborhood was again bustling with people taking walks and walking their animals. Junior adored the girls and the cats, and a fun day was in store for him, as well.

James Middleton had made his morning rounds to Cats Pause Shelter. He had surgically altered one particularly aggressive male stray that had been brought in by a feral cat community volunteer. That will fix not only his aggression, James thought, but his propensity to propagate, as well! Arbor and Syrah sat together on the clinic's reception counter, and they appeared to be smiling in contentment. James couldn't help thinking about the welcome return to calmness in Seven Oaks and he made mental plans to ask Mary when she came to the clinic that afternoon for the pleasure of her company that evening. With the pall of a killer-on-the-loose removed from the community, he had hopes that they would enjoy a wonderful dinner with friends.

The Knightly Ranch had nearly returned to its usual ranch-type normalcy, too. Andrew had found a new horse trainer who had actually been mentored at one time by Donald Jenkins. The young man was eager to prove himself, and the little colt that had given Andrew such a hard time seemed to respect the new trainer. Olivia and the cats had seen the colt calmly nuzzle his new friend who he followed around the corral like a puppy, and the cats then felt free to settle down to mousing duties in the barns. Jaime, Paco and Juan were happy to welcome the new trainer as a contributing member of their ranching family. Paco was relieved that the information he provided would help determine how Donald died, and he would testify in court to that effect. He was looking forward to autumn and greeting his family in the United States.

Charles breathed a sigh of relief that a killer had been apprehended. There were still a few loose ends to wrap up, but all the evidence was properly filed, the grand jury had returned an indictment in Donald's case, and a trial would determine Duke Loma's fate.

Charles was puzzled, though, about several events that occurred along the path to Duke's arrest. He simply couldn't put a finger on why he felt so strongly about Duke's role in Donald's death even before the evidence pointed directly to Loma. He supposed it could be credited to instinct after serving as a law enforcement officer for so many years, but he also felt strongly that it had to be something more. And when Kate would come to him with an insight, she would usually only say she 'had a premonition.' He was a facts man, and relying on instincts made him uncomfortable. Yet, her insights usually proved true. And then, he couldn't shake the feeling that the cats were somehow leading him to discover clues. Puzzling, indeed.

Mo, of course, knew exactly why Kate acted on her feelings and why Charles' instincts were often enhanced. Why, if not for me and my feline friends, thought Mo, no one in this town would ever solve any crime. We cats are natural born sleuths, so to deny listening to *our* instincts would be pure folly.

211

CINCO DE MEOW

Mo sat in the window of Kate's office at Cats Pause and enjoyed the sunshine on her lovely fur. Ahhhh, life is good, she mused. I wonder what tomorrow will bring? At that thought, she bounded off the window sill and raced through the shelter. *It's good to be alive*!

As Mo resumed her duties as liaison between the shelter and the community, she traveled through the shelter to visit every single cat that waited patiently for a human to find them. She promised each of them in turn that it would only be a short while longer until they found human love and their furr-ever homes.

And while I'm helping you search, she thought, I'll keep my eyes open for any ne'er-do-well who may enter here. You can count on me-owww!

CINCO DE MEOW

More

Mo the Shelter Cat Mysteries

by

Maureen Murphy Williams

MAUREEN
MURPHY
WILLIAMS

CAT MAN
DEUX

A MO THE
SHELTER CAT
MYSTERY

Shrieking and howling in a makeshift cage, Mo arrived unceremoniously with police escort at Cats Pause Feline Shelter. In the quiet wine-country township of Seven Oaks, Oregon, where drama is beating a parking ticket or recovering a tipped glass of pinot noir, Mo's 'mum' has been murdered! Suddenly orphaned and facing life as a shelter cat, Mo enlists new-found shelter feline friends, Phillip, Edward and Diana, to help find mum's killer. Mo, though, must keep a secret she feels will bring harm to her new friends, so she teams up with shelter director, Kate Ferguson, to uncover who did the deed. Kate and Mo investigate why a group of California investors is secretly trying to acquire valuable vineyard land. Through links with the community and the local police, they discover the intent of the buy-up is to rezone the farmlands to develop mega-housing, and destroy the delicate ecosystem and wine producing promise of the Jory Hills AVA. A surprise discovery leads them down a path of intrigue and betrayal; by exposing the plot to ruin the land, they expose the murderer.

MAUREEN MURPHY WILLIAMS

CATASTROPHE

A Mo the Shelter Cat Mystery

WINERY
ENTRANCE
→

Even the baby raccoons appeared huge to the cats as they shrank to the far corners of their temporary apartments at Cats Pause Feline Shelter. The felines' one objective: avoid the invaders' furry little hands that reached between the narrow bars for leftover cat dinner – lest they become part of the raccoons' diet, too. *Mum, save me!* Mo silently pleaded to her human companion Kate, who was at this hour several miles away and sleeping soundly. Good grief, thought Kate as she sat bolt upright in bed, her head spinning, her eyes blurry from sleep. What is going on at the shelter? Mo reserves telepathy for dire emergencies, and she is most certainly sending a distress signal. Kate jumped out of bed and began dressing warmly for her trek into the Oregon winter night. Although Kate knew something was terribly amiss from Mo's frantic pleas, she couldn't know that a raccoon invasion had occurred at the shelter – and that a grisly murder had been committed there as well!

Maureen Murphy Williams' cat detective series, *Mo the Shelter Cat Mysteries*, was inspired by the adoption of Morgan, who spent three years in local shelters awaiting her furr-ever home. Maureen's passion for animal welfare and her love of Oregon wine country are paired to bring a new flavor to the cat mystery genre. Maureen resides in Portland with Morgan, and three other rescued cats, Mona, Mac and Murphy, portrayed in Seven Oaks as the domesticated feral family of Commissioner George King.

www.ingramcontent.com/pod-product-compliance
Lightning Source LLC
Chambersburg PA
CBHW070612130626
46556CB00001B/347